MY ELBERT

My Elbert

KAREN DROPPS

SPRING CEDARS®

Cover art by Andrea Crane
Author photo by Ashley Allen
Book design by Spring Cedars

ISBN 978-1-963117-36-3 (paperback)
ISBN 978-1-963117-37-0 (hardback)
ISBN 978-1-963117-38-7 (ebook)

Published by Spring Cedars
Denver, Colorado
www.springcedars.com

Table of Contents

There once was a man from Nantucket,
Who kept all his cash in a bucket.
Then one day,
His wife had her say,
And as for the bucket, she took it.

Chapter 1

There once was a man from Nantucket… Isn't that how all great stories start? The thing is the rest of that original limerick is not all that bad, yet when the first line is uttered, people jump out of their skin with ick because of the rewritten raunchy rhymes. But I know the rest, and it involves money, deceit, and of all things, a bucket. Who am I, you may ask? Well, I am the wife who ran away and, though many heard I left the bucket on Nantucket, I took that too. It all started many moons ago on the small island of Nantucket. The man was Elbert, and what called him there was the sea.

My name is Zilla Harper; I was born and raised on Nantucket. My ancestors came to this island in the summer of 1641, and we have been here ever since. The women of our family have always been house minders and mothers; the men of our family have always been preachers, brought here by the Anglican Church to minister to the island. The other men on the island are whalers and are not much in the way of God-fearing individuals. They live by a code, and it does not match with the Harper minister's code. Our family preaches the ways of Jesus Christ, whereas the whalers worship and live by the ways of the sea.

It was my father's aim that I continue the tradition of all the Harper women before me: marry a minister and tend to the needs of a family and the island. Therefore, it became my goal to find a man—a minister—marry, and start this ideal family. But as I grew older and wiser, I realized the men who worshiped the sea may have the right idea. I longed to find my liberty, and I thought that in finding the love of my life, I would also find my escape from the island.

So, sit around and hear the story of how I found my man…and freedom.

Chapter 2

The tavern was a stuffy place with wooden tables and chairs that may have been there since it opened back in 1680–one of the first places built here on the island. It had a smell of low tide any local could describe, with a mix of stale ale, a musk which reeked of salt and death. To some, it was an aphrodisiac. Many a night, my friends and I sat around discussing the men who wafted this smell throughout the room. To us, it was the ocean's cologne, and we were powerless to it. I had become a regular at the tavern, sitting at my usual table, hoping the scent of low tide would bring my chance.

I met my chance with Elbert. He was fresh off his boat and wanted all who were in the tavern that night to know he had caught the big one. Big what? Well, he was a whaler, and he had gotten his big pay; it was as big as they come out in the ocean, and he was proudly spreading the word around town. This enormous whale was his meal ticket, and that of many others as well.

I heard rumors that Elbert had been the captain of a whaling ship out of another port, New Bedford. It was said that he walked around New Bedford with an air of the best of the best, and that the mainland was too small for him. He soon acquired his own ship and headed for Nantucket. This new ship, as he described it, was the greatest ship ever built, just like the man at its helm. Elbert hired a small crew to help him bring in the biggest catch out there: whales.

Most evenings, he held court in the tavern. He became a local hero to many, as whaling had had less success in the past few years. He had the attention of most of the patrons and regaled those that he could with a dramatic recreation of his exploits. The stories changed nightly, but they always ended the same: "I had that whale in my sights, and I knew it was him or me, and I knew I had to fight."

It was on one of these nights, when I heard him tell his tales, that I fell head over heels for him. I knew he was the love of my life.

Chapter 3

You may wonder why a daughter of a minister was at a tavern on a cold night, or how I was even allowed to be in such a place of ill repute. Well, it wasn't simple.

I was to marry a man whom my father approved of, named Brenton. He was a minister and was chosen to take over the church on my father's retirement, and to be my husband. But Brenton was not the type of man who could survive on a harsh island such as Nantucket. He was fresh from England and spent his life in the luxuries of the upper class, growing up on the large estate of his uncle. When he became of age, Brenton was sent to the seminary to begin his training as a minister. When completed, he hoped to be placed in a nice parish in the country, where he could maintain his lifestyle, but he was sent over to the colonies to start his missionary work.

He was first placed in the shoe factory town of Stoughton, where the boots outnumbered the men. It was the boot capital of New England. Brenton went there to change the minds of the men and women in town, but found there was little he could do, as they fought among themselves over which church would reign. The Methodists were in a battle with the Universalists over who would be the First Parish of the town. Families were being split by this schism; the son of the Methodist minister joined the Universalist Church, and soon all of Stoughton was divided. Brenton was left on the outskirts with his small flock of Anglican followers. After only a year, he was reassigned to my little island of Nantucket.

Brenton arrived in November 1835; it was cold, and the weather had produced some precipitation. It was hard to tell if it was snow, rain, or sleet; all that could be determined was that it was cold and wet. It was this coldness that could bring the strongest man to shiver, and Brenton was nowhere near the strongest man.

Father and I went to the pier to meet his ship. He walked onto the land with a shiver and a stumble, clothed in the highest fashion of the day—which was made for a warmer climate. He stuck out like a sore thumb that had caught itself in the proverbial pie.

Nonetheless, Brenton was welcomed into our home and started his ministry a few weeks later. Our house was typical of New England, one which started small—just a room or two—and expanded over time. With this method, houses tended to be a mixed bag of rooms and halls. Our kitchen was in the cellar. Mother always said it was easier this way since the coal could be delivered right next to the stove; there was an entrance down a few stairs from the back of the house. The main floor had the parlor where we greeted guests, Father's study, and the dining room. There was a narrow staircase between the kitchen and dining room, which helped with moving dishes up and down. The bedrooms were upstairs, mine was next to my parents, and there was an empty one at the end of the hall. It was a warm and inviting place that always felt like a home more than a house.

Mother liked Brenton enough and let him join us for meals after he was moved into an apartment next to the church. He and Father had lively discussions on scripture, and he seemed to want to learn more about our little island. He would go to the pier to speak with the fishermen about religion and philosophy. All of them thought him to be just another preacher trying to get them to change their ways; they listened and shrugged off whatever damning he had for them that day.

Brenton was trying to fit the mold that he thought a preacher was supposed to be, but he did not realize that here on Nantucket, we have our own views of ministers. Father tried to show him that their job was to support families through the tough months, not lecture them on scripture. But Brenton, being an upper-class gentleman, was stubborn and thought that his ways were best. In his mind, converting the entire island was his ticket off Nantucket. But this was a losing fight, as Father would spend countless hours dissuading him.

After about six months, Brenton was asked to dinner one night, and my parents put their master plan in motion: Father had decided Brenton would be an acceptable replacement for himself as minister and a suitable mate for me.

Our guest showed up at exactly six o'clock that evening, dressed in his finest threads, as he did any night he was invited over. I met him at the door with a smile and a gentle greeting. As was the plan, this man was to be my husband, so I tried to be cordial with him. Brenton was tall, with eyes like the ocean and hair like hay. He had a face like a god. Any woman would be lucky to be seen on his arm.

It was a warm Nantucket summer night and his tall stature swayed in the wind of an oncoming storm. He was welcomed in and offered a libation to tide him over until our meal. He declined, as was his policy. Father, Mother, Brenton, and I sat in the parlor looking out of the bay window that had a view over the ocean. We were having a colorful conversation about Genesis and the order of how the earth was formed when we adjourned to the table. Mother had prepared the usual feast for those who lived in a fishing village: fish and potatoes.

My mother used to be a cook for an aristocratic family in Boston; she was an amazing cook, and I could tell she missed the grind of a large household. Since Mother did most of the cooking in the family, we employed a servant, Katherine. She was my nanny growing up and now cleaned and helped with other tasks throughout the house and the church. She lived in an apartment in our attic, which she beautifully made her own over the years.

As we prayed before being served our feast, there was an air of uncertainty. It could have been the weather, or it may have been that I knew my life was about to change. Father stood, held his glass out for a toast, and stated that after careful review, he was ready to hand over his congregation to Brenton and hoped that our families would one day be more connected. As Father took his seat, I glanced at Brenton and watched him turn green. Being the gentleman that he was, he sat through the rest of the meal and, at the end, pardoned himself with a weak excuse of an early morning. He slinked out into the dark. After that night, we seldom saw Brenton around the house, or even around town.

A month had passed, and my mother approached me to take some food to Brenton and check in on him. I knocked on the door to his new residence above the local grocers, expecting to be turned away. He asked me in. As I walked into his charming three-room apartment, I was invited to sit in one of two fashionable armchairs facing a grand fireplace. Brenton went to the adjacent kitchen to fetch us some tea. I sat in this refinement and pondered how a man on Nantucket could have such stylish furniture and décor. I was puzzled further when he brought in a tray of China fit for a queen, or at least a prince who was next in line to the throne. Such extravagances were unknown on our small island, especially in the house of a minister. He sat down to join me for a cup of tea and started to explain some things.

Brenton came from the estate of a wealthy uncle in a small county in central England. His mother died in childbirth, and no one knew who his father was. From birth, he was taken to his mother's favorite brother until he came of age, sixteen, and was sent to the seminary. There, he realized this life was not for him. He did what he was told, waiting for the day he would inherit his uncle's estate. His uncle never married, never had children, and Brenton was the closest thing he had to a son.

Brenton did his time and accepted placement in a large city. He was sent to Manchester in northern England. It was not London, but it did have its fashionable side. He ran his congregation as well as he could, still waiting for his chance to escape back to the country. After a year in Manchester, he was sent to America to look after congregations in Massachusetts. The elders of the church thought his refinement would be an asset to the colonies. He reluctantly took the position, biding his time until he would receive his inheritance. But his uncle was at the peak of health.

When Brenton was sent to Nantucket, he expected it would be an easy placement. The rumor mill of ministers had buzzed that my father's work was a cakewalk that many others had enjoyed. He had heard that my father was a good man who had grown and nurtured the island's congregation. He thought if he impressed him, he could find a way to get back to England and closer to his home in the country.

Brenton did not wish ill on his uncle; he wanted to show him he was capable of being a minister, that he could change the minds of the fishermen. He hoped success on the island would prove to his uncle that he could be helpful in the little hamlet outside his estate. Brenton wrote to his uncle repeatedly but was told to keep at it on Nantucket and he would be sent for soon enough.

When Father announced he wanted Brenton to take over for him, Brenton saw his whole life plan fade away. And that was why he stayed away, hoping Father would see that he was not, in fact, ready to take over the church. Brenton desperately wanted to return to England. As for Father wanting him to join the family and become my husband, Brenton revealed to me a personal secret that he swore no other person knew. To protect our bond, I took this secret to my grave. However, I could say that Brenton was not inclined to marry anytime soon.

As I listened to his story, I had an eye-opening moment. I decided to be vulnerable in return and tell him something I had kept from my family: I had no intention of marrying a minister and hoped my future husband would be a sailor or merchant who would provide me the adventure and freedom I so desired. He agreed to keep my secret, and together we constructed a plan for how to move forward.

We would act as if we were going through with Father's plan, but in the meantime, I would help find Brenton a better placement back in England. I had met missionaries and traveling ministers over the years and kept in touch with many of their families. So, I would write to them, making a plea to help Brenton return home to his ailing uncle. None of it was a lie. Brenton's uncle was aging and had expressed wanting to spend more time with his nephew, his only living relative. While Brenton was keen on receiving that inheritance, he still loved his uncle as a father.

For the next six months, Brenton and I acted like he was going to take over for Father, and after that, he was going to marry me. I wrote every day to different ministers and waited patiently for our plan to work. One cold November day, I received word that a friend of mine in Thurmaston had an open position in his congregation. He was eager to have some help at his church and had been looking for the right candidate. I brought the letter to Brenton, and we prepared to complete our mission.

That evening, I invited Brenton to tea. He arrived promptly at four, and I escorted him into our parlor. As we sat and sipped tea, Father and Mother joined us. We chatted, and then, in the most courtly of ways, Brenton asked if he could share some news with the family.

Brenton related to Mother and Father that since he was raised by his uncle, who was getting older, he always hoped to go back to Thurmaston so he could return the help his uncle had given him in raising him. Brenton thanked my parents for all their guidance; he would never forget his time on the island.

I caught a glimpse of Father smiling, but fear stood behind his eyes as he realized his grand plan had fallen to the wayside. Father mentioned he knew the minister in Thurmaston and would send a letter of reference speaking to Brenton's exceptional work here on Nantucket. Brenton thanked him and turned to me, putting the second half of our plan into motion.

He dropped to one knee and, in jest, asked if I would join him in England and take up the post of his wife and partner. My parents looked like small children waiting to hear if they could have cake for dinner.

As quickly as he had asked, I answered, and sadly, my parents received neither cake nor a son-in-law. I could not follow him, as I was needed on the island, and Nantucket would always be my home. We shared a subtle wink and nearly took a bow for our accomplished performance. Brenton was free, and soon I would be tasting my own freedom.

Over the next few weeks, I helped Brenton pack up his things for his journey back to England. We spent many of those days laughing and joking about how we were able to escape from the futures that had nearly befallen us; our scheme had worked. It was near the new year when Brenton's ship was set to depart. That morning, he made his way to the pier, and I met him there along with Father and Mother. Mother had created a basket with food for his long trip across the ocean. We said our goodbyes and asked him to write often. We watched him sail off, and with that, the chapter of Brenton came to an end. A new story for me was about to start.

Chapter 4

Father wrote to the governing body of our church for a replacement. It was after the fifth letter when he finally received the reply he was waiting for. This new man, in my father's eyes, was supposed to be the next candidate to be my husband. I still did not wish to continue in the family tradition of marrying a minister and spending the rest of my life serving my husband's ministry. But I waited in anticipation to see who my potential husband was to be. His name was Arthur Smith.

In early May, I went to the pier with my parents to greet our new minister to be. When he exited the ship, we realized the governing body had not told us the whole truth. Arthur held the hand of his wife, and two little twin boys followed behind them. Father may have found a replacement for him, but he would not be a husband for me. Arthur and his wife Alice greeted us with warmth and seemed to be a good fit for our small island.

After accompanying the newly arrived family to their housing, they accepted our invitation to dinner that evening. As the sun set, we waited for our guests to arrive; they were not as prompt as our former minister to be, but you could not expect promptness from families with small children. The Smiths arrived, but ten minutes late. I took the boys to play in the backyard until dinner to give their mother a break. Around seven o'clock, we were beckoned to join the rest of the family.

Dinner with the Smiths was delightful. They were a family who had traveled together since the boys were born; Nicholas and William were ten-year-old twins. They were positioned at a church in Central Falls, Rhode Island. But they never felt a connection to such a large city and were looking for a smaller congregation where they could spend the next several decades. When they were asked to go to Nantucket, they jumped at the chance to start anew and relished the idea of being part of an intimate island. They hoped to make a home on Nantucket, to have their boys grow and learn here.

After dinner, the Smiths entertained us with their tales of adventure. They spent time in Peru, where they were part of a congregation that worked with locals. They climbed mountains and learned to speak Spanish and local dialects. They also spent time in India and helped build orphanages there. It seemed they had lived several amazing lives before accepting this new position. Father was impressed. Half of his wish would come true: he would be able to hand over his congregation to Arthur Smith and his family.

Over the next few months, we had regular dinners and teas at the Smiths. They regaled us with more tales, and we told them stories of the fishermen on the island. It was about a year after their arrival when Father proposed to Rev. Smith that he take over for him at the church. With no one surprised, Rev. Smith said yes, and Father started the process of handing over his congregation.

Chapter 5

Over the next several months, Father prepared his protégé to take on the business of running the church. He met with Rev. Smith daily, discussing and planning practices and rituals that were to continue. The big hand-off was fast approaching, and it would take place at the annual Festival of the Whale: a time in late May when the local fishermen paid homage to their gods of the sea and thanked them for supplying the whales that kept them warm in the winter and fed throughout the year.

At this point, the whalers would be returning from sea and the festival was a celebration of their winter voyage, reuniting with family, and the beginning of a new season. The whole island would come together and eat the spoils of spring: clams, mussels, lobster, and scrod. The festival weekend would be filled with family, friends, food, and fun.

On Saturday, I accompanied my parents to the festival with the Smith children in tow. I took them around to dance and play with others while their parents went with Father and Mother to meet with other parishioners. I took the boys by the hand, and we explored the grounds outside the church. We walked by a group of musicians who played a common tune that for the life of me I did not know the name of, but when it started playing, my feet started tapping. The three of us stopped, spun around, and showed off our dance steps. For a moment, I forgot all my troubles and escaped to happier times: I was a child with no care in the world, holding on to my mother's hand, as we too spun and watched the world blur around us.

We moved on to tasting some of the treats prepared by the local women's group, feasting on fried fish and lemonade. Fried fish was special; we prepared fish every which way, but fried was a rarity. We munched away, and then some of the new ladies on the island brought out a new treat for us to try. The ladies were recent immigrants from Europe; they had crossed the Atlantic to Nantucket all the way from Portugal and had brought a recipe with them called malassadas. It seemed to be a piece of dough that was fried in the same oil as the fish. But it was a sweet tooth's heaven.

The boys and I sat under a tree to enjoy the malassadas. We watched the local whalers and fishermen march from the pier to the festival. It was just a few minutes walk away, but it looked as though it would take these men hours. They were worn and weathered. Rumors were running throughout the island that this year had been especially brutal and not very lucrative. But within the crew, there was one man who seemed to celebrate a season of wealth.

The men approached the festival smelling of low tide, which for me was the smell of a real man. The parade of men walking from the pier into town was a chance for everyone to cheer them on and welcome them home. All along the cobblestone streets, women and children waited to see their loved ones return from months at sea. There were tears of joy, and for some, pain. The men would hold a net for each comrade lost at sea. Each net held the earnings and personal effects of the whaler who did not make it back. It was the task of each captain and the youngest of the ship to offer the net to the man's loved ones. It was at that moment some women knew their husband, son, or father was not returning home. Luckily, this year many were spared the pain of loss as there were few nets.

Standing under the tree next to us was Mrs. Ferreira, one of the Portuguese women. She was holding back tears. Mrs. Ferreira was a younger lady and new to the Festival of the Whale. She kept asking where he was and if he was coming. I told her to keep looking and prayed he would appear. I asked what her husband looked like so I could help scan the crowd to find him. I comforted her, saying that since he was new to whaling, it would be his job to walk in the back of the parade.

Finally, we spotted him walking around the corner, carrying a net. His wife collapsed in relief. I explained her husband would have to inform another family that they had lost their man. Mrs. Ferreira looked at me with terror and then newfound purpose.

"I am going to follow my husband and help deliver the tragic news so that the family will not be alone." She felt it was her duty to support those around her.

It was this statement that encompassed what it meant to live on our island: We all worked together as a community. It took a community to build each other up and to thrive; we comforted each other in times of need, and we celebrated our triumphs as one large family.

At the end of the parade, the men stopped at the church where my father and the new minister blessed them and presented a prayer of thanksgiving for a season of success. The men offered their praise to God—some secretly to their own gods—then with their families, they sat outside at long tables filled with seafood galore, every inch covered with food. The eyes of the children opened wide.

The twins had never seen this much food. As we all settled around our table, Rev. Smith and Father quieted the crowd. Before they gave the blessing of the meal, Father took the opportunity to thank the island for all the great years he had had leading the congregation. He reminisced about how welcoming everyone was when he married Mother and how great the community had been in helping him raise his small family.

He then declared, "It is this community that makes the next part of my speech even harder to make. I have been your spiritual leader for over forty years, so it is with a heavy heart that I announce I am stepping down from my position. I have enjoyed every minute of serving each one of you. My ancestors came to Nantucket at its founding in 1641 and established a church for all to worship. We have grown here and have served all that needed help. I am the end of the Harper line, but I feel that Rev. Smith will be a great replacement. Over these months, he has become part of our family. I happily leave this community in his hands and know he will fall in love with this island and you, as I have." To initiate the transfer, he handed over the task of this year's blessing to Rev. Smith.

Our new minister smiled and introduced himself to the men who had been away at sea. He turned to his wife and children, Nicholas and William, and introduced them as well. He then asked everyone to bow their heads and receive the Lord's blessing. All present, from diverse backgrounds, lowered their heads asking their higher being for blessings and thanks for coming home after another whaling season. Rev. Smith raised his glass, toasted the day, and proclaimed us all to enjoy our time of reconnecting.

As we finished our feast, and the day turned into evening, our party began to break up, and we turned to each other to say goodbye. The men took off with their families to play games at the fair with their children. The twins ran with their father and mother toward the ring toss. My parents walked away hand in hand to spend time with the community at their last gathering as leaders.

I was left at the table with empty plates and other maidens. It was up to us, those who had not found love, to pick up after those who had found theirs. We came from all corners of the island, but we leaned on each other and shared in the task left to us with purpose and a bit of levity. Together, we cleaned up while also leaving room for a bit of fun. Who doesn't love a good sponge fight from time to time?

Chapter 6

It took us almost an hour to clean up the feast. When we were done, the sun was going down and the cleanup group watched as the reunited families departed. Their joy filled the air. In the back of my mind, I thought of the families who were going home without a part of themselves, the families that seemed never to be whole again. As they faded from our view, we said our goodbyes, but two of the women followed along with me to the local tavern. After I had failed to fulfill my duty with Brenton, and Rev. Smith was already married, my father allowed me entrance to the tavern to possibly find a husband for myself.

The temperature was crisp that evening, and it started to rain. The cold of a New England spring night had us running down the cobblestone streets. I was at the end of our line and in the night's gaiety, I stepped into an ice-cold puddle. With a freeze, I skipped along with my friends, laughing our way to the warmth of the tavern.

Many of the men from the ships were already a few ales to the wind. Some sat alone at the bar, while others sat at the few tables scattered around the place. We headed to the back by the only heat source, a small wood stove. We hoped that the men who were sitting there would see us, move aside, and let us warm up.

As we made our way, the men's heads turned. We were a new sight for them. When they had left for their journeys six months ago, women could not enter the tavern. It was after most of the men left that the owner and his wife decided women were welcome in their establishment. We were allowed to come in any night, if we conducted ourselves well and sat at a table—sitting at the bar was not acceptable. These rules seemed well advised, and we followed them, though it seemed it was the men who needed the rules. The women were always on their best behavior in the tavern, while the men were a rowdy bunch who had forgotten social rules after months away at sea. It had been quiet when the whalers were gone, but now that they were back, it was loud and full of cheer.

With my two friends by my side, we sat at our table near the stove. Within moments, a young man burst over and tried to claim a stake in our time. We said no thank you and waited for the bartender to come over and take our order. Once our first potential suitor left, only a moment lapsed before the next one came over with the same inquiry. We again politely said no. I caught the eye of the man behind the bar, and he quickly came over, took our order, and gave the men in the room a look with a real clear message: these women are under my care, so watch yourselves!

Mr. Jones was the owner of this establishment. His ancestors came to Nantucket with mine. While we built the local church, his family built the tavern. They named it The Pickled Quail and set up shop just on the edge of town. From the seventeenth century until about six months ago, it was a refuge for the men on the island. Many nights they spent drinking their ales and spouting their stories.

The Jones family passed The Pickled Quail down from generation to generation, much like the parsonage was passed in my family. Although our two families were in different professions, we acted in the same vein. We both listened and passed on advice to those who sought it, though the tavern had the added benefit of a copious supply of alcohol.

When Mr. Jones and his wife Helen a friend from my school days–took over a few years ago from his father, they saw that the dynamics of the island were changing. New groups of immigrants from all walks of life were arriving and bringing their own traditions and social norms. With the changes of the island, The Pickled Quail also evolved. It was around this time that the whaling season was shortened and fewer catches were being made. Helen saw an opportunity and convinced her husband that allowing women in the tavern would give them a safe place to gather, and it would help keep the men in line. She was right. The men fought less in front of the women, and their language cleaned up.

This night was no different. The whalers coming off the ships were rambunctious and lively, but at the sight of women in the tavern, they quickly adjusted their tune and straightened themselves out. As the evening drew on, more and more men filled the room. They ranged from the young who had money to spend, to the middle-aged who had given most of their money to their wives, to the old salt dogs who would happily trade a story for a pint. The more men who came through the door, the louder it got, each one trying to outdo the other with tales of their time at sea.

One man was louder and more expressive than any other. He was tall, dark, and handsome; he was the greatest looking man in The Pickled Quail. As he boasted about his latest adventure, it seemed like he was the only one in the room. My heart stopped beating for a second. I flashed him my biggest smile to steal his glance. As if it were fate, he turned his attention toward me. For the first time in my life, the life of the party—the gorgeous man in the tavern—was looking at me. I could hardly hold on to my excitement. As he swaggered by the other women, we locked eyes and, for that moment, it was just the two of us in the world.

When he joined our table, he offered me his hand. "My name is Elbert, and you are the most beautiful thing I have ever seen."

My cheeks blushed like I had been out in the wind all day. "Hello, my name is Zilla, and I am glad I caught your eye."

He sat down and shared his story through a slur of words, as the whiskey had caught up to him. Elbert was born in Ireland and made his way to America at fourteen by stowing away on a merchant ship. Once in Boston, he made his way to New Bedford, looking for work on a whaling ship. He worked his way up and now owned his own ship. Listening to him speak awakened in me a want for my own adventures. I smiled and dreamed of what adventures I could have if I could go off with him. All I could do was swoon as he told, in great detail, of how he and his crew of five took on a large sperm whale.

They were off the coast of Nantucket when his watchman called out, "Our prize is on the port side." The crew changed course, getting the ship as close as possible to the whale. Elbert lifted his harpoon and threw it with all his might. In a single blow, he struck the majestic beast.

I noticed the size of his arms and imagined the strength they would exert in throwing that harpoon. They were large but comforting, as I imagined myself wrapped up in them.

The whale threw a fit as it tried to get away, but its end was near. The crew was thrilled to have caught a big one and reap their rewards when they would arrive back on shore.

Elbert's story, like many of the others, barely made sense, but after a lifetime among whalers, I knew there was some truth to it, but all would exaggerate the drama of the catch, especially if women were present.

The excitement was palpable at the tavern, for the years of whaling had dragged on, and the chances of catching a whale had dwindled. When a ship came back successful, the whole island came alive again. The evening continued with the ale flowing and the songs lofting on high. It was a time of celebration. Nantucket whalers had gotten their whale, and they had money to burn.

I stayed as long as I could, always with an eye on Elbert. He had taken on a new persona as more liquor flowed. The boasting led to talks of fighting; he went about the place looking for someone to prove his strength.

At one point, he yelled out, "Who is next? No one can beat me. I am the god of the sea!" He climbed on a table and found a broom to hold up as his trident.

This behavior usually appalled me, but with Elbert, it was wonderfully intoxicating. His need to fight others seemed manly and added to his charm. I knew that no suitor my parents brought home could hold a light to the magnificent Captain Elbert. Even saying his name had become the chorus of a love song in my head. That night, I knew he was the man I was going to marry. His charm had won me over. I was smitten like a kitten. I was in love for the first time.

Elbert walked me back to my house, and we said goodnight. He lingered for a moment, seemingly wanting to kiss me, but that would have been a step too far. So I offered him my hand. He held it as we made plans to go for a walk through the marshes the following day, then he kissed my hand and walked away. I stood at the door to watch him saunter down the road. I caught my breath before entering the house and slunk down in a chair in the parlor; I could not gain the energy to make it up to my room. This was a night I would remember forever.

Chapter 7

The sun licked my cheek through the windows of the parlor, and I awoke to a new day. Before I could fully open my eyes, Mother came into the room with an apron tied around her waist, a duster in hand, and a purpose. She was in search of answers. I was barely awake, and she knew I would be at my most vulnerable.

She started by asking why I was sleeping downstairs. I was tempted to tell her about Elbert, but as I was about to open my mouth, I hesitated. She approached with her feathers and started dusting the chair I was sitting in, asking again what I was doing in the chair.

"Are you sick? Did you drink too much last night? Who was with you? What time did you get in?"

Should I let her in on my amazing evening? What would be her reaction? I had told her about other men from the tavern before, and it was always the same conversation. She would drone on about how the quality of the men at that establishment were only interested in my maidenhood, and that they were not the caliber of men that she and Father would approve of; she and Father would find a respectable pastor for me to marry.

While I was considering my answer, she used the largest piece of her arsenal: the triple name.

"Zilla Patrice Harper, why won't you answer me?"

I needed to answer any one of her questions for it all to stop, but I did not want to give away too much. I made the decision that my Elbert would be my secret. I would spend my every waking breath making sure he would be mine, and I would be his. I longed for our walk in the afternoon, for another chance to be in his presence, feeling that warmth again.

I tried to bide my time until Father would come down for breakfast and save me. I gave Mother simple answers, doing my duty to respect her by responding, but I was careful not to divulge too much. I stood up and started to make my way to the door when my reprieve finally walked in. With Father in the parlor, Mother stopped her questioning and hastened to the kitchen, remembering the tea was not ready yet for breakfast. Before heading upstairs to change out of the clothes from the day before, I whispered a thanks to Father, which he returned with a wink.

But at breakfast, the interrogation continued. This time it was Father's turn. I had hardly taken a seat when, in his most calming but accusatory voice, asked, "And what mischief were you up to last night, Zilla?"

I had had time to think about how to answer. "I met a ship's crew who had caught a sperm whale. I spent the night hearing all their stories, and before I knew it, the hour was later than I had realized. When I got home, the house was quiet, and I did not want to wake anyone, so I slept in the chair." I held my secret in my fist, squeezing tight, trying to keep myself from revealing my Elbert.

When I was ready to tell my family about my Elbert, it would be Father first. I found Mother always pestering about the details: Who was that? What was in that letter? Why are you wearing your fine jewelry? I never had any privacy from her. But Father, he asked questions of substance and wanted a conversation.

Soon, breakfast was finished, and I only had three hours to wait until Elbert came. I started to become nervous. I ran up the stairs to change for my walk, and it hit me: How could I hide my Elbert when he was about to knock on our front door? How was I going to keep this secret? A sense of anxiety overtook me, and I found myself breathless.

I needed to be the first to the door, that was certain. I also needed a story if they saw me around town with him, or if people talked. Being the pastor's daughter, everyone on the island knew me, and if they saw me with an unknown man, especially a fisherman, my father would know before I returned to the front door. It had happened many times before, like the day my friend and I skipped school to play down by the docks. I thought I had gotten away with it, but as soon as I came home, there was Father with his arms crossed and a stern look on his face. My plan with Elbert needed to be secure and fool-proof. I knew I could find a way. I had to be with my Elbert and would stop at nothing to make it happen.

Before I could think any more of my predicament, the pitter-patter of feet brought me back to reality. The door swung open, and Nicholas and William Smith came barreling in. I had forgotten that I was teaching them this morning. I found it hard to stay on task as my mind wandered. In one of these wanderings, the twins asked what whaling was all about. I was brought back to the lesson and had found a solution to my problem. If I were to be seen with a ship's captain, I could explain that I was speaking to him on behalf of the twins. It was almost too perfect.

Around noon, the boys' lessons were done, and we headed downstairs for lunch. It was time to lay the groundwork. We sat with Father, and he asked, as he did every day, what my plans were for the afternoon. I informed him that I had an appointment with a whaling captain at the teahouse to discuss his career. Father was a bit confused. Our family had been on Nantucket since its founding, so why would I need to speak to someone about whaling?

Being the daughter of a minister always under the magnifying glass, I had learned how to only give the necessary information and to shape my answers so that they never seemed to be out of place. Like the time when I was still in school and Father saw me walking along the beach. I had crafted a tale that I was on a class assignment to collect seashells for the younger students. Father approved and instructed me to carry on. I used the same tactic today: making the reason plausible. So I explained that I was meeting the captain for tea to discuss the possibility of him speaking with the twins about whaling.

"That seems like a splendid idea! We have so many whalers around, best to get to the source. Good luck today." And then Father reached into his pocket to give me some coins to help pay for tea.

I thanked him and started thinking of all the conversations I would have with my Elbert. A smile covered my entire face.

Chapter 8

I looked at the clock in the foyer. I had a mere one hour to get ready and a thousand things I needed to do. My nerves started to take over, my hands were shaking, and I felt butterflies in my stomach. I had to catch my breath as I considered what to wear for my Elbert.

I opened my wardrobe to pick out a frock. It was a sunny spring day, so I decided that the dark colors would be out. Soon my floor had a pile of burgundy and navy-blue dresses. I searched for what was left and saw a light-yellow frock and a baby-blue one. Yellow always looked nice on me, but this day, with all the sun, I felt it would drown me out. I went to the window to look at the hydrangeas; a baby-blue frock was the best choice.

I slipped it on and, with a quick look in the mirror, declared myself ready. Then I grabbed the small blue flower in my vase and added it to my hair. I felt it was the last piece that was needed to complete the outfit. The flower gave me a sense of ease, reminding me of my childhood when I would pick flowers in the field with Katherine. On Saturdays, Mother would send the two of us out of the house, and Katherine would take me to this lush field at the end of our road. We would run through the field and pick flowers. It was here she introduced me to poetry and other books. The small blue flower in my hair reminded me of those wonderful days.

I glanced at my pocket watch: ten minutes to get to the door before anyone else in the house. I scurried down the stairs and reached the foyer seven minutes before my Elbert would reach the front steps. I waited by the door, counting down the seconds like a girl waiting for that special letter in the mail. My eyes darted between my pocket watch and the grandfather clock in the foyer.

I sat on the small bench by the door—the place where we would take off our snow boots in the winter—and tried to keep myself in perfect condition. I stayed still, wanting not to wrinkle my frock, and as time ticked away, I fiddled with the flower in my hair, worrying that I may have been wrong about our conversation the night before.

As I kept touching the flower to make sure it was there, questions started running through my head. Had I imagined that whole evening? Was my Elbert just a dream? I shifted positions so I could easily see both the clock and the window. When would I see my Elbert walk up that gate? The time ticked on, and soon it was half past the hour. I started to think he was never coming,

I began walking around the room to distract myself and noticed Mother was now a step behind me. I knew she was snooping, trying to see who it was I was meeting. This would ruin my secret. I had to go back to my post so I could intercept my Elbert before she could get her claws into him. I returned to the bench to keep watch on the clock and the window. As it was about to strike two, I felt defeated. I took one last peek out the window before deciding to head upstairs.

There he was. My Elbert. Walking up the lane. I ran outside and slammed the door shut to slow Mother from following behind. When I reached the gate and stood before him, all my anxiety melted away. He greeted me warmly and proposed we go for a walk along the beach. I happily agreed, and we scurried away.

We talked as if we were old friends, discussing our love of the ocean, our fondness for our feet in the sand, and the beauty of sea glass. I went on about what it was like growing up on the island and spent most of the walk pointing out my favorite spots along the way. We soon made it to my favorite beach. It was the best place to watch the sunset since there was no land blocking the view of the horizon. My Elbert seemed to hold on to every word I spoke, and I fell even more in love with him.

We made our way down to the sand. I sat on a rock to remove my shoes and glanced around to be sure no one would see us, but secretly I did not really care. I was in my own world with my Elbert, and there was no one who could break that spell. We walked along the crashing waves as he asked me more questions. It was freeing finding someone who knew very little about me, a rarity being the minister's daughter on such a small island. Halfway down the beach, my Elbert reached down and picked up one of the most beautiful pieces of sea glass I had ever seen. He placed it in my palm. It was as blue as the ocean and perfectly clear. I smiled and thanked him as I slipped it into my pocket.

By this point, I felt I had monopolized the conversation and tried to ask some of my own questions, but he found a way to shrug them off. I took the cue that his past was not something he was open about, so I asked about his future. He became very excited, like a kid anticipating presents on Christmas morning.

"I am going to go back out whaling, of course. This last journey was just the beginning, and that whale was not my last!" he said with much confidence and pride. "My place is on the sea as a captain of a vessel. I know I will never go back to being a deckhand. It is captain or nothing for me."

I asked what he meant to do with his time when not whaling. He lost a bit of his confidence and started to spin a story.

"I will, of course, work on the island somehow, but I will, of course, be the manager or owner of whatever venture I take on." He trailed on like he had not thought of what else there was to do beside whaling. "I'll start a shop that sells equipment for things at sea... But never mind that, I should get you home." With that, his part of sharing ended. He had been tightlipped about his past and had a single vision for the future: whaling.

We sat on a rock and put our shoes back on. All the while, I was keeping an eye out for anyone who would report back to my parents that I was seen with a man without my shoes on. We were in the clear. We started our way home, this time in silence. I noticed we were free of prying eyes, so I reached out my pinky, hoping to touch him. He latched onto it with his, and I felt a warmth and tingle. I was right about what I had felt last night at the tavern. This man was someone who would be a part of my life forever. He had stolen my heart, and my life would never be the same.

We neared home and talked about when we could see each other again. We agreed that we should meet for tea the next day at two o'clock. I wanted to mention that he had been an hour late today, but felt it would upset our perfect day, so I let it go. We reached my gate, and he leaned in to kiss me. This would be a breach of etiquette, so I quickly turned my head, and he kissed my cheek. As he left, I already began counting down the seconds until I would meet my Elbert again.

Chapter 9

I barely made it through the front door when Mother bombarded me with her questions: Who was I with? What was I doing? I reminded her I was meeting with a fisherman captain about coming to talk with the twins. But she wanted to know more.

"Zilla! Where did you go? What did you talk about? Who else was there?"

I knew she would not relent, so I went downstairs to the kitchen, hoping there was something I could do that would get me out of answering. The kitchen had a large stove on one wall and a line of sinks on the other. In the middle was a large wooden table on which Mother prepared all her wonderful meals. As I entered the kitchen, Mother was in hot pursuit. I said what she wanted to hear. "We shared a pot of oolong tea and discussed whaling. May I help with making supper?" Mother handed me a bowl of carrots. I grabbed the knife and started peeling the carrots, waiting for her next set of questions, when Katherine walked in. Unfortunately, this was not a reprieve but another voice to question what I had been doing.

Katherine sat next to me with a bowl of potatoes. "How was your afternoon with the strapping ship captain?"

I almost sliced my finger, not expecting her very blunt question. I put down my knife. "We discussed whaling and shared a pot of oolong tea."

Mother from the other side of the room piped in. "She is a vault, and we are not privy to see in."

This was Mother's way of guilting me into giving more information. I fell for it and obliged. "We also shared some finger sandwiches, and he told me about his life at sea. He is happy to teach the twins more about his work as a captain." This answer seemed to satisfy them both, and we got back to our tasks at hand. When finished, I rushed upstairs to my room to be alone and recapture all the majesty of the walk with my Elbert.

I reached into my pocket, pulled out the piece of sea glass, and held it to the light to see its beautiful colors reflecting on the wall. Then I opened my keepsake box hidden under my bed. It was a plain box with an odd shield at the top. I had bought it from a church sale and liked that it said *Veni Vidi Vici*. It held all my secrets. I placed the sea glass inside and pulled out my diary. I wrote about our walk and mused about how I would sneak out tomorrow. I had used the tearoom as an excuse today, so I would need another story to keep my secret. It was only four o'clock, and I could still get a note out to my friend Teresa. She would be open to helping me out.

Teresa Corriea was my oldest friend. She came to Nantucket from Portugal when she was five. Her family was part of the new wave of whalers who were looking for their big break. These immigrants were of a different religion and had set up their own neighborhood. Though Nantucket was small, the various groups of immigrants who came to the island set up their own villages. The Portuguese built Smooth Hummocks to the south of Town Pasture where the main harbor was. They had their own Catholic church, but all the children went to the same school as the other kids on the island. That was how I met Teresa.

On the first day of school, we sat next to each other and soon became the best of friends. We were known as the mischievous twins. If there was any tomfoolery going on at school, there was a good chance it was the two of us. We once were caught putting chalk in the teacher's eraser so that when she went to erase her work, it would add more chalk. After being scolded by the teacher and our parents, we knew we would be inseparable.

When we finished school, we kept up our friendship and made sure to see each other as often as we could. A few years ago, Teresa met Michael, and in a short time, they were married. As I was not Catholic, I could not stand with her at the wedding, but I was by her side in every other way possible. I knew she would help me with my current predicament. I had helped her when she was first courting Michael. Her parents were not accepting of him as she was from the Azores, and he had lived in America for too long. I had acted as a decoy so they could meet in secret. Now the roles would reverse.

In my note, I needed to let her know to join me at the teahouse, but to meet me here first, and at the same time, I needed to let her know she was part of a larger plot to help me get away with meeting a man my parents had not yet met. In our younger days, we had created our own secret code, with rules outlined in our school book. We had certain phrases we would use that indicated that what was written was only part of the message. I reached into my side table and pulled out the old notebook. The childish handwritten words, TOP SECRET DO NOT READ, adorned the cover.

I opened it up to figure out how best to communicate with her. There were entries saying *boys are cute, let's sneak to the beach after curfew*, and *our mothers are so annoying*. I searched and found the right guise: *yours in fishing*, which meant meet me at my house and help me in my ruse. So I wrote to her to join me for tea tomorrow to catch up on the going on of spring and signed it *Yours in Fishing*, hoping she would check her old book as well. I addressed the note, sealed it, and asked Peter, our driver, if he could deliver the letter to Teresa. He accepted, as he already had an errand to run near there. When he left, I heard Mother calling me to come help in the kitchen.

As I entered, Mother jabbered all the tasks I needed to help with. She asked me to get the potatoes and carrots ready. Katherine and I had peeled them earlier in the day, so there was not much left to do except to boil them. But Mother found a way to critique and correct my cooking.

"Don't overfill the pot, it will boil over!"

I rolled my eyes and answered, "Of course, Mother." She gave me a glaring look and went about getting the chicken ready. This was our routine just about every night: She asked me to do a task and then spent the whole time critiquing it. By the end of our cooking, I reminded her, "You are the one who taught me. I know what I am doing." Tonight was no different, but I understood where it was coming from. Mother shined in the kitchen. It was her sanctuary, and she took pride in all the food that came out of it. I kind of enjoyed our constant bickering and came to cherish those moments in the kitchen doing my part as her apprentice.

We finished our preparations, and Katherine walked in, signaling it was my time to set the table. On my way to the dining room, I ran into Father. He was walking one of his parishioners, Matthew Chatham, to the door and stopped to introduce me. I knew the look Father had on his face. It meant this was a particularly great bachelor—right here in the hallway—with whom to fall in love and have a large brood of children.

Since these types of introductions happened at least once a month, I had a knack for ending them quickly. One time, Father brought over an oaf of a man who smelled like rotten fish. His appearance was not any better. When Father introduced me, I marched toward the door without missing a beat and politely bid the man goodbye, all the while holding my breath.

Matthew Chatham shook my hand; no sparks were felt. I made my regrets and showed him the exit. As I closed the door behind me, I felt a bit of relief that I had avoided another of Father's arrangements.

At dinner, Father said grace, and we tucked in our meal. He started the conversation, talking up his new prospect for me. Matthew was a lawyer, single, and looking to establish himself here on the island. He was gentle and a good Christian. Father insisted I should give him a chance. With a pinch of the finger, a trick I learned many years ago, I was able to nod my way through dinner without letting out my secret. Seeing Father's quest to have me married off sooner than later, I knew I had to keep my secret a bit longer. But maybe Matthew was the solution to my problem. If I kept up dates with him, I could continue to sneak off and see my Elbert.

As we retired to the parlor, I thought of a way to accept my new suitor without being too enthusiastic, as I knew I would at some point have to break it off.

Matthew Chatham was born in Taunton, Massachusetts, the son of a factory owner. Taunton was known as the Silver City, the place where most silver products were made in New England. Matthew's father ran one of these factories and saw a bright future for his son, wanting him to move up the social ladder. As it was, he was a self-made man, part of a growing group of merchants who made their own money as opposed to the ruling class of old money. It was his idea for Matthew to become a lawyer, thus cementing the future of the family.

Matthew was the second born boy in the family, leaving his older brother Stephen to take on the factory and Matthew—the smarter of the two—to become a lawyer. There were still five younger siblings, two boys and three girls; it was on Matthew to be the savior and the cornerstone of the family. When he completed the requisite education, he went on to Harvard University, where he studied law. He interned at a firm in Boston, then chose to strike out on his own. It was at this time that he heard of the need for a lawyer on Nantucket. He was always one for adventure, so he wrote to the firm seeking employment. He arrived just days before meeting my father, still new to island life.

I looked up from my embroidery work and asked Father about Matthew. Mother sat nearby, listening intently. Father obliged, stating that Matthew would be taking over Mr. Franklin's law firm and had come to meet with Father at the request of Mr. Franklin to see if it was acceptable to take over his law firm from a Christian point of view. Mr. Franklin was our most devoted parishioner. This was something he did often. After meeting with Matthew, Father decided to give his blessing.

I asked if Father would mind having him come for lunch this Saturday so I could get to know him better. Mother piped up with excitement; she had the perfect recipe for this lunch and would make it extra special. Father agreed to send him a note with an invitation. With this plan in place, I took my leave and went to bed.

Chapter 10

I woke in a panic, trying to remember all the parts of the plan I had made. Before getting dressed, I sat with my diary to write everything down. I looked at the calendar to see if I was teaching the twins today and sighed in relief that I had the morning free. I then remembered the conversation I had with my parents the night before. I had added Matthew to be my stand-in suitor, and this would be put into place at lunch on Saturday. All the cogs and gears in my mind were working again. Things were looking up, and I got dressed.

As I reached for the door handle, another thought popped into my head. How was I to keep Elbert from the front door? I thought of sending a note for him to meet me at the teahouse, but then it dawned on me. I had no idea where he lived. I didn't even know his last name. I thought through all our conversations to see if there was a clue to where he lived. He had barely spoken about himself. I knew very little of my Elbert.

I was determined in my vision of the future that he would be mine, so today I would get this missing information. What could be another avenue to keep him from getting to the front door? I realized there was a simple solution: I would meet Teresa in the street—she was always punctual—so we could both intercept him at the same time. I felt comfort knowing that she would be with me if he were late, and I could gauge her reaction when initially meeting my future husband.

The clock struck noon, and I readied myself for the afternoon. Everything hinged on perfect timing. It was like a play, and all the characters had their parts to perform, except I had not yet given Teresa her lines. I rushed down the stairs. At the front door, I yelled to Mother that I was on my way out. I waited for Teresa at our meeting spot and looked at my pocket watch. Teresa was never late. I was five minutes early.

There she was, coming around the corner, right on time. Her look said it all: What is Zilla plotting now? I flagged her down.

"And what's my part in all this?" she asked.

I explained her role, and she smiled with excitement. Then we waited for my Elbert. I thought again of how little I knew about him as Teresa asked questions. "I actually don't know," I would answer. I ended the game when I asked about her family and children. Like any mother, she went on a diatribe about how each was excelling in their own ways. I looked at my pocket watch. It was quarter to three, and he still had not shown. Teresa could see I was anxious and offered that the two of us go to tea in any case. I agreed.

Teresa saw him first, coming around the corner. She ran ahead, then shouted, "Sir! Sir! I have a question for you!" He looked confused but, ever the gentleman, stopped to help with her inquiry.

I approached behind, acting as if I had just seen my friend. "Teresa, fancy seeing you here! Oh wow, Elbert, good to see you too! This is my dearest friend Teresa. Teresa, this is Elbert."

They shared pleasantries and as she took her leave, she embraced me and whispered, "What a great lobster." I smiled and agreed with our coded phrase. This was a great man, one who was meant to be a life partner, much like a lobster. As Teresa walked away, I got a better look at him.

He looked stunning in his blue shirt and gray knitted vest. His arm muscles were visible through his shirt. On top of his head was a traditional Irish scally cap. I got lost in his amber eyes, dark hair, and ocean-kissed skin. He was a vision of perfection. I smiled and asked if he was ready to make our way to the teahouse. He had a surprise for me, something I had not anticipated, something I did not fit into my plan. I reluctantly said yes and followed him.

He gave no indication of what we were doing. I just

assumed it was by the pier, since that was the direction we were heading. Beyond that, I was puzzled. We walked until there was nowhere else to go except into the ocean. At the dock, he led me to a whaling ship, *The Monahan*. I assumed it was his ship as we stepped on board, and it hit me again: I don't even know the name of his ship. I was so smitten that I had failed to ask any important questions.

On board, there was a table on the deck with flowers and two glasses. I sat at the table, and he poured Madeira, a lovely Portuguese wine. I stared into his eyes, and all those important questions left my mind. I was, for this moment, the only one in his vision, and he was mine. Then he left, came back with lobster on a plate, and handed me a cracker to start breaking into the crustacean.

Apparently, Elbert did not know the proper way to serve lobster. He was supposed to slice it for me so I would not have to crack the shell, thus avoiding any embarrassment. Soon, I was covered in water and butter, looking very unladylike. But it was so much fun. We discussed things such as the upcoming season for whaling and our favorite foods. But every time I asked one of the important questions, he took control of the conversation and changed the subject. This went on for about an hour until he asked if I would like a tour of his ship.

I was nervous to be led down to the lower decks, but I pushed that voice out of my mind and followed him below. He showed me all the equipment used to catch whales and as we went through the door into his quarters, a shiver came over me. This time I heeded it and asked to leave. Elbert looked confused, but he listened and escorted me back above. He suggested it was time to go and insisted he was too tired to walk me home. So I left, still with no answers to those important questions. I hoped and prayed that no one would see me walking alone in my humiliation.

I took the long route home, thinking the less traveled road would help keep my secret. Anytime I saw someone, I averted my gaze to avoid stopping and chatting. It took hours to get home, or at least that was how long it felt. I snuck into the back door by the kitchen, ran upstairs, changed, and headed back to the kitchen. I saw dinner was ready and braced for my mother's berating. As I approached the dining room, I heard her and Father speaking in whispers. I cracked the door to hear what they were talking about but startled them, so I entered and said good evening. Mother looked flustered.

It was obvious they had something to discuss with me. Mother had cooked a feast which usually happened when there was something amiss, or one of my strapping young suitors was joining us. We said grace, then passed the food around the table. I could barely manage to hold a plate. I took my first bite of the roast, and Father asked how my day was. It was not the usual way he asked. It had another layer to it, like he knew something.

I answered with as little detail as I could, hoping it

would satiate his inquest.

Then Father asked: "How was your tea with Teresa?" He seemed to want to catch me in a lie.

I dodged the question with benign information, but he held strong. "Who was the man you were with, Zilla?"

My mind raced for an explanation. I opened my mouth, but nothing came out.

Mother interjected, "Mrs. White saw you embrace a man! On the street!"

I took a deep breath to calm my nerves. "Well, Mother, Father, the man was that fisherman I told you about yesterday." I tried to keep my composure and not stutter. "He saw Teresa and me as we were walking and stopped us, as he had something to give me." They seemed to believe me. "I had left my handkerchief at the teahouse the previous day, and he was coming to return it. I was so overcome with emotion since it was my favorite handkerchief... The one with the little daisies that you, Mother, made for me this past Christmas. Emotion overcame me, and I gave him a hug for bringing it back. Teresa was with me the whole time. I guess Mrs. White did not see her."

Father seemed satisfied with my answer, while Mother gave me gigantic eyes. She knew I was lying, but she had no evidence to call me out. They continued their mundane conversations, and I relaxed in my chair. I survived yet another round of questioning.

In the parlor, we talked about our evening activities. Father was researching for his next sermon. This was the one part of the service he did not yet feel the new pastor could handle. Mother got to darning socks, but the pile never seemed to get any smaller as she took on darning for any family that needed it. I did my embroidery work, which I offered for free to those on the island in need. We sat and worked in silence as the clock ticked on. It seemed to tick particularly slowly tonight. I looked up from my piece, noticed it had only been ten minutes, and went back to the silence. It was only broken when Katherine came in with a note for me.

It was from my Elbert! He had written to apologize for his actions and hoped we could meet at the tavern tomorrow night, where he would make it up to me. He did not request an answer to his quandary. In any case, I had no way of letting him know if I would show or not; again, unanswered questions. But he had apologized, and I would get to see him tomorrow evening. I shut the letter and returned to my embroidery so as not to spark suspicion.

Mother caught my smile. "Zilla, who is the note from?"

With no hesitation, I said it was Teresa asking if I could meet her at The Pickled Quail tomorrow night to make up for cutting our tea short today. I explained my fictional story of how she was called away when one of her sons was injured.

"Oh no! What happened? Is there anything we can do or send? I hope it is not that fever going around. I do pray he is all right."

I had forgotten my mother's penchant for wanting to help all who needed it. I had in the past mentioned someone's misfortune, and Mother had gone full steam to help. I said, "It was a false alarm, just a young child who missed his mother."

Soon the candles burned down, indicating it was time for us to retire to bed. I made my way upstairs, exhausted from the day's activities, and fell asleep thinking of my Elbert.

Chapter 11

I awoke with a feeling of excitement. I dressed, went downstairs for breakfast, and saw Mother already frazzled at the prospect of having Matthew join us for Saturday's luncheon. This character had not yet been told his lines for my theatrical production, but I knew I could get him on board. Mother had started her planning for our guest of honor. She called it a luncheon, but this multi-course occasion was starting to look like a Roman feast that would last for days. She wanted to serve fish, cheese, chicken, and a beef roast, eleven types of vegetables, and so much more. Not to mention the variety of desserts.

I interjected, asking what I could do to help. She handed me a list and asked that I take Katherine with me to get the last items needed from the market. Father reminded her that this wasn't to be a large to-do, but she was set in her ways. Father and I looked at each other from across the table and giggled as we knew we could not change her mind and it was best to let her have her feast.

I hurried through breakfast, grabbed my hat and coat, and headed out the door with Katherine. Mother had given us quite a list, mostly for specialty fish and cheeses. As we walked into town, Katherine asked about the letter. She wanted to know more about the handsome young man. I blushed and debated if I could count on her as my confidant. She had always been a friend, and I felt I could trust her to keep my secret. Besides, it would be nice to have someone in the house I could confide in. Throughout my childhood, any issue I was having, I knew Katherine would give me honest advice. Like when I was twelve, and I really liked this boy Lawrence. I wanted to write him a card, and Katherine helped me compose it. She never told my parents about my secret crush, and it led to my first kiss.

As we walked along, I regaled her with the past week's whirlwind romance. I talked about our promenade on the beach and how I went to his ship yesterday for a lobster lunch.

"You were alone with him on his ship? Please tell me you kept to your morals."

I reassured her I never went further than I should have. Katherine was a second mother to me, and I tended to follow her advice, sometimes more than my own mother's. Katherine said she would keep my secret, but if he were someone I would not introduce to my parents, then he may not be the man I ought to be with. I told her it was just too early to mention anything, and that I was planning on meeting him at the tavern tonight. I would consider bringing him by sometime next week. She seemed reassured, and we went along, chatting about the upcoming feast Mother was making and if she could ever top it in the future.

We went about the market, gathering all the ingredients. It took longer than expected. We searched high and low for shallots, finally claimed defeat, and hastened home. When we returned, Mother was in a cooking frenzy. We handed off the items and asked what else we could do to help. We were instructed to set the table with the good silver; Mother was hoping Matthew would notice that our silver was from his father's company.

My father was already in the dining room, put to work shining the silver, which he was not accustomed to. He asked if we could take over, and he would set the table. I took the cloth and silver polish and worked my magic on those tarnished pieces, as they were rarely used. As I finished each piece, Father and Katherine added them to the table. When it felt like I had cleaned all the silver in Buckingham Palace, I asked Mother again what I could do to help, and she sent me to my room to put on my best dress. I obliged.

I reemerged in my finest frock, a wonderful green piece. Not a moment out of my room, there was Mother barking orders.

"Zilla, go stand by the door to greet our guest, make sure you do not blush, and please, act ladylike."

I walked to the door and waited for our guest. He was supposed to arrive at one o'clock. I looked at my pocket watch. Ten minutes. Five minutes before one, he came to the door, flowers in hand. I did my duty and escorted him into the parlor. Mother and Father were already seated, with high hopes, trying their hardest to appear casual. But they looked more like dolls. I took my seat next to Father, and Matthew sat between Mother and me.

We were deep in conversation when Katherine came in. It took a moment for everyone to notice she was there. She informed us that lunch was ready. We entered the dining room to a feast meant for royalty, as if we were back under British rule. Mother had not held back. Matthew kept the conversation going, talking about growing up in Taunton among the factories, about his time in Cambridge attending Harvard, and about how he took up his position here on the island. He was intelligent and well spoken, but he could not hold a candle to my Elbert.

We finished the feast, and Mother had us retreat to the parlor for tea and dessert. I had no room left for more food, but I obliged. As we walked to the parlor, I noticed the clock; I would need to leave in about a half hour to make it to the tavern in time. I started to panic but remembered that I had an excuse. My parents knew I was meeting my friend Teresa. We finished our tea, and I made my excuses.

Father had other plans. As it was getting dark, he had the grand idea that Matthew should take me. I felt a bit of dread until I realized the benefit of having an approved escort. I agreed, as did Matthew. He had told us at dinner that he wanted an opportunity to meet other locals. He gave his thanks, said goodbye, and we departed.

Matthew and I walked along, getting to know each other a bit more. When we were a block from The Pickled Quail, I remembered the other part of my plan for the night. I spent the next few minutes filling him in on Elbert. Matthew assured me he would help me out. He then told me of his own tale. When he was at Harvard, he had fallen in love with a French woman whom he knew his parents would never approve of. He had used a decoy girlfriend to stop his parents from setting him up with a family friend they always loved to have over.

As we reached the door of the tavern, we shook on our agreement to help each other out. He would act like my boyfriend, and I would help introduce him to the island. I saw this as the start of a wonderful friendship. It was six o'clock when we entered, the exact time I was to meet Elbert. I looked around the room, there were the usuals up at the bar, men I had seen in passing, but no Elbert. I noticed an empty table in the back that had a good vantage point of the entrance. I sat, and Matthew went to the bar to get us both a drink, an ale for him, a sherry for me. Matthew chatted with a few gentlemen, and I kept an eye on the door, wondering when my Elbert would arrive.

Matthew returned with my drink and offered to sit with me while I waited. I tried to protest.

"That's what friends are for!" he retorted, sitting down. He tried to start up a conversation with me, but I could not concentrate. I was nervous and kept looking around. "I'm sure he just got caught up with something on his ship. You know how those men of the sea are about their ships, always tinkering."

I felt a small sense of relief and glanced at my pocket watch to see how late he was this time. It read seven o'clock, a whole hour late–and a whole sherry as well. Suddenly, Elbert came bursting through the door with a plethora of men in tow. He looked as if he had been drinking for hours. He must have been drinking on his own since the tavern was the only place that served alcohol on the island. I stopped overthinking it because now he was here.

Matthew caught my blush and joked with me, whispering, "Is that him?" He soon realized it was no joke, so he flagged down Elbert to help me connect with him.

It looked like Elbert thought he was a well-wisher wanting to buy him a drink, but as he came about to our table and saw me sitting there, he became enraged. "She's Mine! She's Mine! Zilla is mine!"

I was horrified and honored at the same time. He was calling me his, but his loud outburst was something that should have scared me away. But I was in love.

Matthew, who I had not realized was a full head taller than Elbert, stood up and assured Elbert that he was only sitting with his friend while she waited. As a gentleman, he apologized and shot me a look.

I understood he was a wave away and would gladly step in if needed. I smiled, thanked him for his company, and encouraged Elbert to sit with me.

Elbert began to go on and on about this large catch on his last trip, the same story he had told me several times.

"There I was, five miles off the coast of Block Island, and I saw a whale!"

The size of the whale and distance always changed, but tonight, he was two sheets to the wind by this point, so his story was more incoherent rambling. His breath smelled like stale whiskey and death. I listened, and when he finished, I took my leave. He begged me to stay and enjoy the night. He offered to fight any man in the tavern for my entertainment, but I was tired after a long day and excused myself. I grabbed my coat and slipped outside.

Nantucket was a safe island and walking home alone was something I had done many times before. I always stayed on the main paths and knew which streets to avoid. I was comfortable on my own, and I preferred to be alone, especially tonight. I had a great time with Matthew; I was happy to include him as my friend. Elbert was showing me who he was little by little, but I seemed to know more about

Matthew after only one afternoon.

I did not know what to think about this. Before I could produce an answer, I heard someone yell my name. I turned around and saw Matthew. I stopped and waited for him to catch up with me. He offered to walk me home. I declined, but he insisted, saying my father would never approve of him not walking me back. I shot him a friendly smile, and we continued getting to know each other.

At home, he extended a friendly handshake, and we said goodbye. I opened the front door, hoping no one was still awake. As I headed to the stairs, I saw Father was still in his study, so I popped my head in to let him know I had returned. He asked how my evening with Matthew went, and I gave him a quick overview, mentioning that he walked me home. Satisfied with my answer, he wished me a good night. I went to my room and lay in bed, dreaming of what it would have been like if Elbert had walked me home.

Chapter 12

Sunday went by with no word from Elbert. I went to services, and Mother invited Matthew to sit in our pew. Father gave a sermon on kindness and bringing kindness to our community, no matter the background of the person. My mind kept straying to all that happened last night. I thought of how Elbert had professed to all around that I was his girl. I thought of his loudness and his tavern drunkenness. I thought about how kind Matthew had been, but that was overshadowed by my wanting to be Elbert's love. The rest of the day was quiet with our normal routine of Sunday roast and an early evening. I waited for word from my Elbert, but alas, it never came.

I awoke the next morning to a knock on my door. I had forgotten that I had lessons with Nicholas and William Smith. I opened the door, yawned, and let them jump on my bed while I changed into a frock. I decided to take the boys to the pier to look at the boats. Mother suggested I bring Katherine with me for some backup, and I agreed. The four of us put on our coats and headed to the pier.

Along the way, we sang songs and pointed out interesting plants and flowers, and soon we arrived. I noticed *The Monahan* in its slip. I kept staring at it, hoping my Elbert would emerge from below deck.

Katherine poked my shoulder to gain my attention. "Is that his ship?"

I could not answer with words and just nodded my head. We watched the twins run up and down the pier, then we roamed to the beach. We picked up shells and beach glass. The children loved finding special shells, wondering what different animals used to live in them. We were all enjoying our time together when a familiar voice called out to me. I stopped in my tracks. Which version of Elbert would show, and how would I hide him from the twins?

I turned to Katherine, asked her to keep an eye on the boys, then ran to greet my Elbert. He gave me an embrace and apologized for how he acted on Saturday night. I accepted his apology and asked why he was here. He said he noticed me on the beach on his way to the market and saw it as fate that he would have a chance to try again with me. I reminded him that Saturday night he had told all in the tavern that I was his girl, and that it had made me happy. We talked of nothingness until I needed to return to the children. He asked if I would meet him for dinner that evening. I wavered in my response, remembering his outburst on Saturday, but I was in love and agreed.

On the way home, I filled Katherine in on what happened Saturday night and our plans for this evening to meet for dinner at The Lucky Compass, a local eatery that was suitable for courting men and women. Again, she warned me that knowing so little but trusting so much was dangerous. I assured her I knew what I was doing and would be careful, then I asked for her help with getting out of the house. I needed a reason to sneak out to meet him, plus a story about why I was out to dinner with someone my parents did not know. Katherine agreed to hand me a letter written from Matthew asking me to meet him for dinner at five o'clock. Hopefully, this bit of trickery would work.

Around lunchtime, as I was helping set the table, Katherine came in and handed me the note. I gave my greatest performance. Mother was as happy as I was pretending to be. With her permission, I wrote a response saying yes, and handed it over to Katherine. After lunch, I went to the parlor to read, and at three o'clock, I headed upstairs to make myself presentable for the evening.

I chose a deep purple frock that I had been told brought out the beauty of my eyes. Next, I thought about what jewelry to wear. I had a string of pearls that I liked to bring out for special occasions. It was a gift from one of my aunts. She always said that a woman was never fully dressed without a string of pearls, and so she gifted a set to each woman in the family upon completing school. I put on the pearls, and they added much charm to the outfit. I grabbed my purse and a shawl for the walk home, and I raced out of the house.

I waited outside the restaurant. He was to meet me at five o'clock, and when I heard the bells ringing, I looked around for him. Again, he was late. I decided I needed to ask the tough questions tonight. I needed to know the real Elbert. I mentally listed all the questions I needed answers to: his full name, his background, where was he from, who were his parents, and more about his ship. I needed to ask: What games did you play as a child? Why did you leave your homeland, actually what was your homeland like?

I kept myself motivated by repeating these questions over and over in my head, all the while looking at my pocket watch, waiting impatiently for him to arrive. At half past five, he strolled up the road and waved. For a moment, I forgot I needed answers and was just happy to see my Elbert. He embraced me, and we walked hand in hand into The Lucky Compass; we were quickly seated. I took a deep breath and out came, "What is your last name?"

He got flustered. "My name is Elbert Monahan."

"Why did you keep it a secret?"

"I thought you would not want to be with me since I am Irish. I was always told that American women turn their noses up at an Irishman."

I reassured him that his nationality was not an issue, and that I liked him for him. I almost said love but did not want to seem too desperate. He ordered for the two of us, and we shared a bottle of wine. I continued with my list of questions. He was from Ireland, from a large Catholic clan. He was to take over the clan and its lands when his father died, but he ran away from this responsibility and landed in Dublin. It was in Dublin that he met a captain who took him under his wing and taught him about whaling and fishing. He soon stowed away and made his escape to New England. I had heard about his adventure from this point on, so saw no need to interrogate further.

After he opened up to me, I knew I had his heart, and he had mine. We spent the rest of the meal talking about mundane things, such as the price of carrots and the unseasonable weather. We acted like an old couple speaking about the little things in life. At the end of the evening, he helped me with my shawl and escorted me out. As we said our goodbyes, he asked if he could meet my parents. I panicked. They thought I had been out with Matthew all night and that I was falling for him; this would be a blow to their plans. I had been keeping Elbert to myself, but if I were to ever make him truly mine, they would have to meet.

I agreed for them to meet at lunch on Saturday, giving me enough time to come up with my next scheme. I wanted to press the issue of his tardiness, but I had already pushed a lot today, so I kept my mouth shut. I would send a note of details, which led to the last question of the night: "Where should I send the note?"

He smiled and said I would figure it out, leaving me with yet another mystery to solve.

Chapter 13

How would I explain my Elbert to my parents, and how would I get him an invitation to luncheon on Saturday? The play was becoming more elaborate, and now all the characters would have to learn new lines. I thought it best to first speak with Katherine, as she was already in on it. I rushed downstairs to the kitchen to find her cleaning up. I snatched a towel to help her dry the dishes and whispered that Elbert wanted to meet my parents.

She dropped the plate. "Are you sure?"

We spent the time to wash the last of the dishes to come up with a plan of how to let my parents know that this past week I had been meeting with a Catholic whaling captain, and how to get him an invitation to Saturday's luncheon. The picture was bleak.

Katherine and I agreed that tomorrow morning at breakfast would be a reasonable time to tell them, as they may not be fully awake yet and may agree without too many questions. Inviting Teresa and her husband Michael to luncheon would be an easy way to ease some of the stress on everyone as well. I also considered inviting Matthew, but remembered his harsh encounter with Elbert at the tavern. I thanked Katherine for the help, bid her a good evening, and joined my parents in the parlor for our evening activities.

As I worked on my embroidery, I concocted my script, imagining what my parents would say in return. Running through these scenes over and over made me anxious, and I started to lose hope of ever being able to tell them. But I had to see this through if I were to have a future with my Elbert. After I finished my work, I excused myself to bed. I grabbed my journal and wrote what I hoped to say at breakfast. After an hour of revising my speech, I had found the right lines and put down my pen. I slowly drifted off to sleep.

I woke early the next day, dressed, and ran downstairs to get to the table before my parents. When I saw they were not up yet, I went down to the kitchen to see if I could help Katherine with breakfast. I shared with her what I had come up with the night before and, after some editing, we worked out the perfect speech. A few minutes later, I was sitting at the table with Mother and Father. I waited while they poured their tea. As they took their first sips, I broke the silence.

"Mother, Father, I have a confession to make. I have

been seeing a man that I met at the tavern. His name is Elbert Monahan, and he is captain of his own whaling ship. We met last week and have fallen for each other and are looking toward our future. I am sorry that I lied to you. I just wanted to make sure this was real before letting you know about him. I would like to invite him to the luncheon on Saturday. I could also invite Teresa and her husband to round out the party."

I waited an eternity for an answer. Mother stared at her teacup and would not look up. Father was the first to speak. He wanted to know more about Captain Monahan. I told him all that I knew, and he agreed to meet him on Saturday. Mother still had not spoken a word; she looked over her glasses in a familiar way that meant I had messed up, and she was disappointed with me.

Finally, Mother raised an eyebrow. She had that look, the one most children have seen, the one that says she knows there was more to my story, but she had no proof. She would be the hardest to convince. The best thing to do was to leave, so I asked to be excused. When granted, I pushed back my seat, grabbed my plate, and made my way to the kitchen.

I filled Katherine in on what had transpired. She and I both agreed it went well, and that I should prepare for when Mother was ready to share her opinion on the matter. Mother and Father left to go about their duties for the day, and I helped Katherine clean the dining room. When finished, Katherine handed me the shopping list and bags. Wednesday shopping was a tradition that Teresa and I had for more than a decade, ever since our mothers trusted us to do it for them.

When I arrived at the market, Teresa was waiting for me, and she knew something was up. "Zilla, what is it this time, and who do I need to kill?" she asked as we hugged.

"Well... A lot has happened since last week." I filled her in about Matthew and the tavern. Then I dropped the big reveal. "Elbert is coming to lunch Saturday."

Teresa was silent for a moment, picking her jaw off the floor. "Why did you tell them so early?"

"Well, he kind of begged to meet them. That has to be a good thing, right?"

"Our parents want what's best for us. Worse case, you can run away together!"

We chuckled, although it did seem appealing. We walked along, picking up our groceries, talking about what Mother's delayed action might be.

"She might serve stale bread and water," Teresa suggested.

"He will probably have to eat down in the kitchen." I laughed, knowing it would not be the same massive feast from last week. "Why don't you and your husband join us on Saturday? Mother always loves having you over, and it will cut some of the tension." Teresa agreed, and we got onto the next question: How do we get a message to him? We found a bench to brainstorm.

"Well, where does he live?"

I paused and looked at the ground. Teresa knew this meant I did not know the answer.

As a true friend, she shot me a look of disappointment. "Zilla! You're in love with this man, and you don't know where he lives?"

"Umm, yeah, I know his ship, and that he likes to go to the tavern... He is also Catholic. Maybe he lives in your neighborhood?"

"The Irish have their own church and neighborhood. They wouldn't be in contact with the Portuguese."

With no solution in sight, and a need to get back to our respective homes, we said our goodbyes and agreed to meet for tea the next day. I returned home just in time for lunch. After eating, I excused myself to my room so I could write the invitation in peace. I took out the finest paper and wrote—with my best penmanship—an invitation that my Elbert could not refuse. As my pen danced, I imagined our future: We would move into a small home just outside of town; we would have a widow's walk for me to look out on the harbor, pining for my lover, hoping that he was coming home safe and soon. I rhythmically added one o'clock to the invite and thought of what our reunions after his lengthy times at sea would be like.

I was so filled with joy that I had lost track of time.

It was getting dark, and I was being called for supper. I tucked the invite in my diary and rushed downstairs to join my family at the table, along with Matthew, to my surprise. We greeted each other as I took my seat. He leaned over to ask how things were going, and I rolled my eyes in such a way that he knew we would need to speak later.

As we ate, Mother asked Matthew about his days and plans for the week, waiting for him to reveal that he had nowhere to go on Saturday, and she could invite him. I needed a moment to let Matthew know that under no circumstances was he to come to the luncheon. He needed to know that this was when my parents would meet Elbert for the first time. But alas, I was stuck by etiquette, sitting and listening to Mother speaking. As the meal dragged on, her attempts became more desperate. When we finished, she just extended the invitation once and for all. I nervously looked at Matthew; he needed to reject this invitation. He understood and politely declined. I felt instant relief. My plan was still intact for now. Matthew and I retreated to the parlor while Mother insisted Father help her clean up.

I relayed to Matthew the whole luncheon debacle. He let out a bit of laughter. "I figured something was up when your mother appeared at my office with an invitation for supper tonight on such short notice."

I thanked him for his refusal of the Saturday invitation, as it would be awkward with both him and Elbert at the same luncheon.

He agreed, but issued a friendly warning. "Zilla, please be wary. Elbert does not seem to be who he says he is."

I understood his concern, but had no worries. We moved on from talking about my Elbert to milder topics. We were discussing the lack of potatoes at the market when Mother and Father joined. Father handed Matthew a glass of brandy, and they settled in a corner to discuss manly things. Mother and I poured ourselves some sherry and went to the other side of the room.

That was when she started prying me with questions: "So, what else are you hiding? Do you have other secrets, a secret job? Family? Friends? Where is it you go during the day? Who is this man we are bringing into our home? Is he kind? Who are his parents? Where was he raised?"

She wanted to know everything, and she knew I could not leave, or it would be rude to our guest. I answered as best I could, realizing again how little I knew of Elbert, except for the fact he had stolen my heart. Mother was annoyed and unsatisfied, but soon relented in her questions. I was relieved when the evening ended. I walked Matthew to the door and thanked him again for all the help.

"That's what friends are for. I'll always be there for you."

Chapter 14

The next morning, I enlisted the help of Katherine to get the invitation to Captain Elbert Monahan. I had added a special message and sealed it with a kiss and a spray of my perfume. I still had no way of knowing where he would be day to day, so I asked that Katherine deliver it to his ship. It was the most logical place to find him.

Today, I was in charge of the twins, and it was perfect weather to explore the marshes. I had always loved being out in the marshes hunting for different creatures. When we arrived, I taught the children about frogs, fish, and tidal pools. It was a fun and messy morning. We made our way back to my home for lunch with our parents and as we entered the gate, Mother instructed us to go around the back to clean up first. We obliged.

The boys were famished and excited to have lunch in the kitchen with Katherine. I was to eat in the dining room with the other adults. Katherine tried to grab me to let me know how everything went, but Nicholas and William were asking for her, and I was already late for lunch upstairs. I ran up to meet my parents and the Smiths and extended my apologies for the delay.

It was a pleasant time. Mr. and Mrs. Smith were closer to my age than my parents' age, and they had wonderful stories of their work throughout the world. It made me a bit jealous that I had never yet traveled off the island; I had always wanted to see the world. Maybe Elbert would take me on his ship, and we could explore foreign lands together.

I made plans to help Nicholas and William for two days next week. After lunch, Katherine took me aside to give me an update. She had checked in on his ship, but he was not there, so when she was in the hardware store, she asked where she might find the captain of *The Monahan*. Someone said they had seen him at the tavern every night.

I had to go to the tavern tonight, and I needed to find someone to come with me. I tried Katherine, but she declined, stating that she was not one to go to a tavern and wanted a quiet evening. I thought of Teresa, but evenings were for her growing family now. This left me with one other option: Matthew. Last time my Elbert saw me with Matthew, he became jealous. Nonetheless, I went to Matthew's office to ask if he wanted to accompany me.

I trudged along the road, reviewing the plans for Saturday and running through how I would ask Matthew to come with me. I took a deep breath, walked up the stairs to his office, and opened the door. Inside sat his receptionist Maria, one of Teresa's sisters whom I had become friends with over the years. We exchanged pleasantries, and I asked to speak with Matthew.

She returned with her boss, and before we could go back to the privacy of his office, I blurted out my theatrical production. Matthew took a moment to think and came up with an additional act: We would invite Maria to help keep Elbert's jealousy at bay. She was excited to be included, as she rarely had an opportunity to enjoy an evening out. We talked a little longer and agreed on meeting at eight o'clock at the tavern.

That night, at dinner, Mother and Father asked questions about who I was meeting and why I was going out. I stayed calm and explained that I was to meet Matthew and Maria. With their approval, I ran upstairs to change into an impressive frock and put on my pearls.

I arrived at The Pickled Quail five minutes before eight. As I walked to the door, right behind me were Matthew and Maria. We entered together and found a table at the back. I had the invitation letter tucked away in my bag, touching it over and over, making sure I had not forgotten it. We got our drinks and gossiped about all that was happening on the island. I kept one eye on the door, waiting for my Elbert to appear. At about nine o'clock, he walked in, boisterous as ever. I waited until he noticed me to slip him his invite for Saturday.

Time slowed, waiting for my love to notice me. Finally, though only maybe ten minutes, we locked eyes, and he proclaimed to all present that his lady was here. My heart skipped a beat; hearing him call me his lady made me so happy, and it caused me to blush. My Elbert came over to the table to join us.

He spent the evening in control of the conversation, telling us of his many adventures, which almost seemed like fantasy. "The whale was fifty feet!" And even more unbelievable: "I single-handedly steered my ship and aimed the spear gun, going as fast as I could. I threw that spear and turned the helm at the same time!"

After an hour of his ongoing storytelling, it was the end of the night for me. I made my excuses and handed him my invitation with a wink and a smile. He leaned in to kiss me, but I knew it would get around town that I allowed him to kiss me in public, so I turned my cheek; his kiss landed there instead.

"Am I not owed at least a kiss?"

I smiled and thanked him for the evening, ignoring his frustration as a sign that he was just as in love with me as I was with him. It was easy to shake off anything negative. He was my dream come true! I replayed the evening the whole walk home. I was so smitten, everything he did seemed like a romantic gesture. I was in love. I could not wait to take the next steps with my Elbert.

Chapter 15

Saturday came quickly. Mother and Katherine were up early preparing for our guests in the kitchen. This week's luncheon would be a much smaller feast than our last one, which spoke volumes of how Mother perceived me bringing a man she had not pre approved. Instead of seven main courses, she made one roast with only three sides, not eleven. The scaled-down lunch felt like a slight to my Elbert, but I knew that once Mother got to know him, she would change her mind.

I had already done my part by setting the table and was staying out of their way until needed. I went up to change only minutes before Teresa arrived. As I had requested, she and her husband Michael came an hour early. Michael looked lost standing at the door, so I yelled down the stairs that Father was in his study and would not mind company. He was off in a flash.

Teresa ran up the stairs to help me prepare. Like a

true friend, she gave her honest opinion of the red dress I had picked. After some discussion, we both agreed that my light blue dress with small flowers in my hair was the perfect outfit. We looked at the time and realized we needed to pick up the pace. I powdered my nose, Teresa pinned up my hair in this year's style, and we sprinted downstairs.

In the parlor, we found Father and Michael in a heated discussion, which dissipated when Teresa and I joined.

"Weather seems to be changing," Michael said.

Father joined in on the benign subject. "Ah yes, can never tell if one day to the next will be cold or hot."

Teresa added, "The sun is bright today. Hopefully, it will hold out for the weekend."

The clock struck one, and my heart skipped a beat. I listened for a knock at the door, announcing his arrival. Soon the chimes were done, but still no knock. We continued our pleasant chatter, but I was unfocused. I kept one ear to the door and one eye on the small clock on the mantel. Moments kept passing and still no knock. I saw Mother's look. It was one of disappointment; she was a stickler for time. She always used the phrase: To be early is to be on time, to be on time is to be late, to be late is unacceptable. I already knew Elbert did not abide by this phrase. I watched the minutes tick by until the clock showed thirty minutes past the hour. Mother declared we would start lunch, and when our other guest arrived, he could join us.

As we walked to the dining room, there was a knock on the door. Katherine got there first and greeted him in. There was my Elbert, standing in all his handsomeness. One look at his smile, and I could forget about his faults. He sat across from me at the table and next to Michael. My heart fluttered, but my stomach turned as I thought of what was about to happen. What kind of questions would my parents ask? I could see the gears turning in my mother's mind. She would be the hard hitter, and Father would ask more philosophical questions. Thank God Teresa was there. She would know when to step in with her own questions to keep peace in the room. As Father led us in grace, I peered up to see my Elbert looking lovingly at me, and I knew everything would be fine.

The food was served, we tucked in for our meal, and Mother started the inquisition. "So, Elbert, tell us about you, your family? Parents?"

"My father passed away around ten years ago. Last I heard, my mother is still alive in County Cork, but the mail is slow between the island and Ireland. I am the oldest of twelve siblings, ten girls and two boys. Mother still lives with the younger ones. I send money and news as often as I can."

Mother nodded her head in approval, and I noted the new details he provided.

Father was next. His initial questions, as usual, were

about religion. As a man of the cloth, he asked, "Where do you worship?"

Elbert seemed caught off guard by this question. He stumbled a bit. "I was raised Catholic, but being at sea makes it hard to attend regularly."

Teresa chimed in, "Michael and I both attend the Catholic Church, and when it comes to the fishermen, they are more lenient."

Father looked at me, perplexed. I interjected, asking Mother if the potatoes were a new recipe; she loved to experiment and loved it even more when someone noticed. This tactic worked as she began a tangent about the new spices that had arrived from overseas, and how she had been changing things up with them. I sighed a bit, like a light breeze through the trees, and smiled at my Elbert, which he returned with a thank you nod. The rest of the meal went by with little drama.

We all retreated to the parlor across the hall for tea and dessert; Mother had made her famous crumpets. We talked of simple things, and I could tell Elbert was feeling comfortable as he started taking control of the conversation.

"There I was, ten miles off the coast of Block Island, and I could see the behemoth of a creature come up for air. I called my crew, and we made haste toward the whale…"

I enjoyed hearing him talk of his exploits at sea and

looked around the room to see if others were as enthralled. Father, Teresa, and Michael appeared interested, while Mother seemed annoyed. But overall, Elbert was making the impression I was hoping for. As we wrapped up the afternoon, Teresa and Michael took their leave first. When Elbert stood, he had an aura of victory about him, like he had conquered another whale.

I walked him to the door, and when he saw no one was looking, he leaned in and we embraced in our first kiss; I could not resist it this time. It was magical. I felt lighter than air. He smiled and asked if we could meet for a walk on Monday; he would come by to pick me up at two. He said he would have a question for me and hoped I would say yes. I melted into that moment.

Chapter 16

It was our typical Sunday. We went to church, and Father, who would not give up the pulpit, gave his sermon. It seemed to be spawned from our luncheon the day before. He spoke of acceptance of others and welcoming other religions into our fold, for Nantucket was a community of many faiths. He raised his voice and raised his arms as he talked about all the different people we had living on the island.

"For example, the Catholics are accepting of the time men go fishing and whaling. Accepting each other makes us a stronger community. We should embrace our differences and find common ground to create a better Nantucket." He emphasized his point again. "When we work together, we not only make ourselves stronger, but we also make the community stronger."

Father struck a chord, and many shouted an Amen in agreement. The new pastor looked on in awe, and some parishioners clapped at the end. Father had an exceptional talent for bringing the scriptures to life, and today was another triumph. After the service, we retired to our home with Matthew in tow. Mother could not bear him all alone on the sabbath and invited him to join us for our Sunday roast.

Matthew walked next to me, and I let him in on all the details from yesterday's luncheon, even the big news that my Elbert had a special question for me tomorrow.

He was excited, but added another warning. "I think Elbert is a good guy, but I have a feeling he is hiding something."

I reassured him I knew in my heart, no matter what the secret, he was the love of my life. I could barely sleep that night thinking about the big mystery question. Tomorrow afternoon, my whole life would change. When I finally fell asleep, it was pitch black outside. All I dreamed about was my Elbert and our future.

Early in the morning, I was the only one awake. Down in the kitchen, I started the water for tea and got the stove going. I was part way through the breakfast routine when Katherine arrived. She was surprised to see me and apologized, saying she thought she was early. I returned the apology, as was customary, and told her I was up early and thought I would help. We worked together to get breakfast on the table, and she asked why I was up.

I could not contain myself. I blurted it all out.

Katherine was shocked. Her face said it all. It was one of dismay and confusion. "How long have you known him?"

It had only been two weeks.

"Zilla! How much do you know about him?"

I paused, then assured her I knew all I needed to know. But I still felt uneasy with her questions, as they did make me wonder if I knew enough about him. I told myself that would all come with time; I loved him, and nothing else mattered. We continued to work in silence. Soon, Mother and Father joined us. We wanted to keep this from them. There was no sense in getting them worked up over an unknown question. I got about my tasks for the morning and, before I knew it, the afternoon had arrived. My Elbert would be here in an hour.

I went upstairs to change into the perfect dress for the occasion, one that was given to me for Christmas a few years ago. It was covered with my favorite flower, daisies, with a light blue background. When I had opened the gift, I had a feeling that I would save this dress for a moment I knew I would never want to forget. I had been keeping it for a special moment, and this was it. I picked the perfect hat and pins to go with the dress and made myself beautiful, all for my Elbert.

I waited in the front hallway until it was two, and as the clock chimed the time, my heart raced. I kept my vigilance; the clock read quarter past the hour, and I was still waiting, hoping that this time would be different. I started thinking about how much a watch cost, and if it was insulting to get him one to help him be on time. At every noise, I perked up, a squirrel, and then a bird, but none of these were my Elbert. The clock now showed half past the hour. A dog barked, which indicated that someone was coming. This time, it was him. I wanted to run out to say hello, but I composed myself and waited for him to arrive. Within moments, he was knocking on the door.

We walked to the shore and looked at the boats coming in. I tried focusing on the moment but began analyzing every movement, waiting for him to ask me the question. We made our way to the beach, the same beach where we had our first outing together, and we removed our shoes to walk barefoot in the sand. For the first time since I met him, he seemed nervous. He grabbed my hand, and we strolled down the beach. Then he stopped and drew a heart in the sand with our initials in it.

"Now when the waves are carried in, our love will go on with the waves forever." He smiled and got down on one knee.

I gasped and almost fainted as he pulled a ring out of his pocket. I started to cry, waiting for him to say the words. I was transported to another world, one that was just the two of us. Nothing else seemed real.

"Zilla, I may have only known you for two weeks, but I know in my heart that you are the woman I want to spend the rest of my life with. Will you do me the honor of being my wife?"

"Yes!" Tears were running down my face. I felt like I was, for the first time, truly happy. I could not wait to get home and share the news. My Elbert was now going to be mine, and we were going to be together for the rest of our lives.

We walked home and talked about sharing the news of our engagement with my parents. My Elbert had done the right thing approaching Father after church to ask for his blessing. Mother was going to be our struggle. We decided to make our way to Teresa's house and let her know first, as she had been in on the relationship since the beginning. We got to her doorstep and heard the pitter-patter of little children. We knocked and a few moments later, she came to the door with a child in tow. We apologized for intruding and said we had news. I showed her my ring, which was a simple band with an emerald stone in the middle and two small diamonds on either side. We both shrieked with excitement. She invited us in to talk about it, but we declined, knowing we needed to make our way to my home. I promised to stop by tomorrow, and she wished us luck with my parents.

Hand in hand with my Elbert, we chatted about our plans for the wedding and how we were going to tell my mother. I suggested I speak to her alone. He stopped a moment at the front gate, and I turned to inquire what was the matter. Without a word, he pulled me in close and gave me the most romantic kiss. He wrapped his strong arms around my waist. I could smell the ocean on his skin. Our lips embraced, and again it was just the two of us in the world.

He said, "I wanted to remember how much I love you before we go into the den of lions."

I chuckled, and we made our way into the house. At this time in the afternoon, Father would be in his study researching for his next sermon or catching up on the paperwork of the church. When we approached the door, it was closed. I looked at my Elbert, smiled, and knocked.

"Who is it?"

"It is me, Father, with Elbert."

"Elbert who?"

Elbert seemed perturbed. I whispered he was just joking.

"Come in, come in, don't mind the mess. I got caught up in some scripture." Father cleared two chairs. "Sit, sit." He kept repeating this while frantically trying to find spots for all his papers.

We sat, and I started tapping my foot as I was nervous about how he would react.

Father stopped clearing and sat at his desk. "What can I do for you?"

"Mr. Harper, I know I have only known your daughter for a short time, but I love her very much. As you know, I asked for her hand in marriage, and she accepted."

Father folded his hands, readjusted his reading glasses, and answered, "Okay."

And that was it. My Elbert was surprised. But I knew that this one-word answer was the best response we could get. Father stood and offered Elbert a drink, and the two started discussing this and that. I saw my opportunity to inform Mother, and I excused myself down to the kitchen.

"Good luck, sweetheart," Father said.

I bumped into Katherine, and she asked if I was all right. I pulled her aside. "I'm engaged!"

"That's fantastic! Let's talk more later. I need to get back to my duties. Your Mother is in the kitchen, and she is in a good mood. Good luck!"

I gave her my thanks. When I got to the top of the stairs, I paused. Reality hit me; I was going to marry the love of my life. My Elbert was going to be mine. I just had to tell my mother. I took my time walking down the stairs. At the door of the kitchen, I paused again, rehearsing my lines.

"Are you just going to stand there, or are you going to help?"

Startled, I went to the stove and took the spoon that Mother was offering and started to stir the sauce. I stared into the pot, waiting for the courage to tell her the news.

She broke the silence. "Who was it you came home with? I heard two voices."

This was my chance. "Elbert came back with me. He is in the study with Father." It was now or never, so I jumped in feet first. "And we are going to get married." I waited in fear for her answer.

The silence was deafening. She finally spoke. "I'm glad, my dear. Let's hope for a long engagement so we have ample time to plan."

Where were the questions, hurtful words, the yelling? This was something I never expected. Mother was onboard with my pending nuptials. What a relief. She instructed me to go upstairs and set the table for four. I bowed to my mother before I walked out the door.

When I finished setting the table, I went into the study to check on the men. They both had their noses in books. I cleared my throat to get their attention and announced that dinner would be in a few minutes and Mother invited Elbert to join. With nods of approval, I left to help Mother and Katherine bring the food to the dining room.

What a wonderful feeling it was to not hide my Elbert anymore; I also felt joy that my dream of being Elbert's wife was well on its way to fruition. We all sat at the table for the first of many family dinners. There was an air of lightness throughout the room. After dinner, Elbert waited for me to finish helping Mother and Katherine clean up so we could both head to the tavern to let his shipmates in on our exciting announcement. We walked hand in hand out into the night.

We found a quiet table in the corner, and Elbert went to the bar to get us our drinks. I scanned the room for whomever I could share my life-changing news with, and I saw Matthew. He came over at the same time my Elbert returned with our drinks. The two exchanged pleasantries, and then I told Matthew of our engagement. He seemed cheerful for us and offered to buy the next round. Maria soon arrived and joined as well. The four of us celebrated as the drinks kept pouring.

As Elbert consumed more alcohol, he started to change his behavior. First, it was his stories at sea becoming more and more ridiculous. As he told it, the whale was anywhere between fifty to five hundred feet long. Then he turned angry, hearing any word out of Matthew's mouth as an invitation for a fight.

Matthew asked, "Would anyone like another round?"

Offended, Elbert quipped, "You think I can't order my own drink? I'm Elbert Monahan, I caught the biggest whale! What have you done?"

He became aggressive as his other personality took over, like a doll with two faces, one that was happy, the other angry. Elbert had shown me this side before. It came out when he was drinking. He would get competitive, argumentative, and rude. Tonight was no different. On his third drink, he tried to start a physical fight with Matthew.

He boasted he could take on anyone, especially a "wimpy lawyer."

Matthew did not take the bait, so Elbert went on to the next table, looking for someone to accept his challenge. After two tables ignored him, the third, which was filled with fellow whalers, gave in. Soon enough, there was an all-out brawl. Fists were flying everywhere. I took to hiding under the table with Maria.

Matthew stepped up to help break the fight. When he gained control of Elbert, he ushered him to the door like a father removing a problem child. Maria and I gathered our things and followed them out the door. Elbert wanted to walk me home. He had a black eye and a split lip; he was stumbling drunk and was in no condition to be seen by my parents. I declined his offer. Maria and I decided to stick together the rest of the night while Matthew would help Elbert home. We went our separate ways.

When Maria and I arrived at my home, we went to my room and settled in for an old-fashioned girls overnight. We discussed what my dream wedding would be like and what my dress would look like. I had heard Queen Victoria wore a simple white dress with flowers in her hair, and I hungered to emulate it. I wanted to be married by my father and have Teresa, Maria, and Katherine as my attendants. We giggled the night away, speaking only of happy things, as to forget about the tense evening.

Chapter 17

The next morning, Maria needed to head off to work early, and I decided to bring Matthew a thank you gift for helping last night. I packed up some of Katherine's famous muffins and headed out the door with Maria.

As we made our way up the street, Maria let me know she kept an extra set of clothes in a bag under her desk so she would be nice and fresh for the new day. I asked her about what it was like working for Matthew. She said it was a breath of fresh air compared to the old man who used to run the firm. Matthew was helpful and never had an angry word for her. It was a comfort knowing my friend had a great place to work with such a kind person.

As we were about to enter the office, Maria stopped for a moment. "Can I be frank, Zilla?"

I nodded my head.

"Is Elbert the man you imagined in your dream wedding?"

I assured her that Elbert was the right man for me. This would not be the first time a friend had concerns, but I always explained away any of his inappropriate behavior. Was I making excuses? No way, in my heart, I knew he was the one.

We walked into Matthew's office, but he was not there. I put the basket of muffins on his desk and wrote a quick note of thanks for all his help. I extended my gratitude to Maria for staying overnight, looked at the clock, and hurried home. The twins were coming over to learn about gardening. I made it back with only moments to grab my gardening apron before the two boys came running up the path.

I enjoyed these lessons. The twins had always lived in large cities and were eager to learn about country life. Living on an island made one self-sufficient. Relying only on the course of the seas made it hard to have consistent supplies, so many locals had vegetable gardens, chickens, and even goats. We learned early on that if there was something we needed, we would make it ourselves; we grew, pickled, and canned most of our food to hold us over winter when supplies were scarce. Today, the twins and I would harvest the cucumbers. Since the Smiths had arrived after planting season, we would be sharing our harvest with them.

The twins were eager to get their hands dirty, and soon we had collected several baskets full of the cucumbers that were ripe enough. Next, we went through the back door to the kitchen to pickle and can them. Every step was a new experience for the twins and they were filled with enthusiasm. In a few hours, we had twelve jars of pickles, and I packed up six for the boys to take home.

I got them cleaned up and ready to leave when Katherine asked me to make a few stops on the way back; she handed me a list. Then, Mother came into the kitchen to see what to prepare for dinner. She saw the list and added a few more items. The list was getting long, so I suggested Katherine come with me. Mother agreed.

With the twins in tow, Katherine and I walked to town, playing games and singing. As we skipped down the road, my eyes caught sight of my Elbert. His bruises from last night were more prominent, and you could tell from a distance that he had been in a tussle. I smiled and waved, but he kept his head down. Was he ignoring me, or had he really not seen me?

Katherine caught me waving, then noticed my mood change. "Is that Elbert? What happened to him?"

I shrugged off the question and continued playing a game with the twins. Within a few minutes, we were at the Smith's house, handing off the boys and our newly canned pickles. On the way to the market, I made small talk with Katherine to curb further questions. Katherine understood I would not talk about Elbert's physical condition and instead, she asked about my wedding plans. Grounded again, I spun the engagement ring on my finger and rambled on about all my ideas for the wedding. Katherine listened and offered to make my dress, which I immediately agreed to; she made the best dresses.

At the market, we split the list to finish in a timely manner. After about an hour, we met up again and started back home. We walked in silence, knowing everything had been said earlier. We got to the kitchen just in time for Mother to hand out our next assignments.

The night passed with little excitement; we ate dinner, went to the parlor, and I worked on my embroidery. The sun retreated, and soon I made my way to my bedroom. It had been a very busy last twenty-four hours: I accepted a proposal from a captain and started planning our wedding; I introduced him to my parents and friends— my secret was out; I also saw him bait and get into a bar fight. I had seen this side of him before, yet still my heart was his, and his alone.

Chapter 18

A few months later, the wedding planning was in full swing. We decided on a date in April so we could have the reception in my parents' backyard and it would not interfere with the whaling season. It was the end of March and things started to change. Spring had sprung, and I was out looking at options for flowers. I was to meet my Elbert afterward to go over the ceremony. By now I had learned how to handle his constant lateness, adjusting the time I told him by thirty minutes so he would show up closer to the right time. I chose daisies and bluebells, then made my way to the church.

Father and Mother were already there waiting. Elbert came soon after. We sat down to go over the details. Father always helped plan wedding ceremonies for couples who wanted to be married in his church. Elbert and I were no different, except we also had Mother in on our meeting. She had convinced Father to include her after quite a bit of pestering.

Father took this opportunity to ask where we were to live after the ceremony. This was supposed to be a simple question, but it was something we had never discussed. I looked at my Elbert and tried to judge what he would say. I was not expecting his answer.

"Zilla will stay with you in your home when I am at sea, and I expect to join her when I return."

My parents' faces turned white; their plans of being the two of them had raced out the door. But they agreed that we were to live as one family under one house. Then Mother asked the questions she had been eagerly sitting on: Did we want children, and which faith would we raise them? I looked again at my Elbert and smiled, hoping he was on my side and wanted to have many children, all raised in the Anglican faith.

Elbert said, "Children are out of the picture."

My heart sank into my stomach. I heard a crash in my mind, as if a china cabinet had fallen, but it wasn't tea cups. It was my dreams of the future. Mother looked just as heartbroken. Father was speechless. I added this to the list of things I could fix after the wedding and changed the subject.

Our wedding ceremony was to start at ten o'clock in the morning. I had chosen Teresa as my matron of honor, and Elbert had not yet said who would be his best man. Father needed to know and inquired who he had chosen.

Elbert stuttered.

"Perhaps Matthew would be a good fit?"

Elbert agreed, and soon we were done with Father's meeting. We walked outside the church and I reached for my Elbert's hand. He pulled it away and asked if he could skip the rest of the wedding planning this afternoon.

I was surprised, he had not been much of a help and had just unilaterally decided what our lives would be. I was hoping we could discuss these things more throughout the day.

"I have an opportunity to get back out to sea and have to leave the day after the wedding."

Another shock. I knew he would have to leave for his next voyage, but thought he would wait at least a week before abandoning his new wife. "You really have to leave the day after the wedding? Couldn't you delay it a bit?"

"Of course I can't. I am the captain, and I said that's the day we have to leave, so that is when we are going. It has to do with tides and things that you would not understand."

I was taken aback. He would deny me children, he would decide where we live, and now he had to leave the day after our wedding? I felt the tears, wanting to yell and cry at the same time. It took all my strength to hold everything back.

I guess this was part of being a captain's wife. Like my mother, who had her role as the pastor's wife, I had my role as well. I knew Elbert would be on his ship for months at a time, and I would run our household by myself, the sort of independence I craved. But it seemed all I was doing was making sacrifices left and right. Was it too much to ask for a few days of normalcy as a married couple before he went off on his voyage? Through gritted teeth and a fake smile to hide my disappointment, I replied, "That's fine, sweetheart, maybe we can meet tonight at the tavern so I can fill you in on the rest of the wedding plans, and you can fill me in on your progress."

He agreed and kissed my check. "Goodbye, I will see you later."

As I hurried to the local baker to try out wedding cakes, I ran into Teresa. She never could resist dessert and graciously offered to assist. We caught up on all the gossip of the day and tried many flavors. We decided on a lemon chiffon cake with white frosting. She assured me the nerves I was feeling were normal, that her husband had had little to no interest in the planning part of their wedding either, and that if I loved Elbert, it would end up being a magnificent wedding and a long, happy marriage.

We split up after the bakery, and I walked slowly home, dreading yet another inquisition from my parents, as there were bound to be additional questions after our counseling session. But soon these questions would be over. I would be Mrs. Monahan, and their control would end.

Chapter 19

I walked in the door just as dinner was being brought to the table. I took off my coat and stepped in to help. After grace was said and food was passed around, Father cleared his throat, "Was staying at home your idea?"

The first round of questions had begun.

Mother piled on. "Why would your soon-to-be husband want you to stay here? Why would he not want a place for you to grow as a family?"

I made sure to have a large scoop of food in my mouth so I had time to compose an answer that sounded plausible. If I said the truth, Father would refuse to marry us. He had always been a firm believer in marriage as the joining of equals, not a husband gaining a wife.

"It won't be forever, Father, it's just that he goes off to sea the day after the wedding and wants me to be comfortable and not have to handle all that goes into finding a home and furnishing it." It wouldn't be a permanent thing. I was sure when my Elbert returned, we would immediately start looking for a place of our own. I took another large bite of chicken, knowing more pushback was coming.

Mother wanted to know if I would persuade him to reconsider children. I took my time chewing and swallowing to come up with a response that would ease her mind so she wouldn't have to keep asking where her grandchildren were. "He meant not in the immediate future. Since we are to live with you, we do not want to add to your burden with another mouth to feed."

Mother looked like she had more to add, but Father cleared his throat, indicating to her to drop the subject. We continued our dinner in silence. We all knew that in two weeks our lives were going to change; I hoped it was for the better. My parents seemed to only see the worse.

After dinner, I bundled up, grabbed my shawl, and set out to The Pickled Quail. It was one of those spring nights with the feeling of snow in the air. The wind was coming off the ocean, sending a spray that blanketed the island in a cold dew. I hastened my step and made it to the tavern in record time. I snuck in, took off the damp layers, made my way to a table in the corner, and waited for my Elbert. He sprung through the door at around eight o'clock. I waved him down, but he went straight to the bar.

I waited at the table, thinking he wanted a drink first, then he would join me. Time ticked by, and still, he did not come. Perhaps he had not seen me? It was improper for a woman to approach the bar, but I approached anyway. His angry voice echoed as he talked to the bartender; my Elbert did not have a good day. I cleared my throat and offered to buy his drink. He smiled and kissed my cheek. I was the key to his happiness and he to mine. He clutched my hand and accompanied me back to the table with our drinks.

Elbert revealed to me he had little luck finding a crew for his next voyage. He had asked around, but few wanted to join him. I listened to his issues, knowing that my place was as a listener; I reminded myself that as his wife-to-be, this would be my role, and tonight was great practice for the future. So, for the next half hour, I listened to his issues. He went on about how hard it was to find good men for his crew. Whenever he came across someone, they were quickly snapped up by another captain. He felt that someone must have been bad talking him through the island, and he was determined to destroy whoever was doing it.

I reached out a hand and comforted him: It was going to be okay. There was never a shortage of whalers on Nantucket. His expression confirmed that my job was done. I told him of my day and running into Teresa. He was glad she had helped pick out a cake and liked the one I had chosen. We spent the rest of the night staring into each other's eyes until it was time for me to head home.

It was nights like these that I looked forward to, where we were open and shared with each other. I wrapped myself up, and my Elbert walked me home. The first snowflakes were falling. It was a magical sign, as snow made everything new again. I giggled, and he smiled as he took my hand. We walked in tandem all the way to my door. After a quick kiss goodbye, we made plans to meet in a few days for lunch. That night, I slept better than I had in a long time. I felt calm; I knew we could make it, and that it was my destiny to be by his side.

The next two weeks flew by. I had my final dress fitting. I had taken a cue from Queen Victoria and went with a white dress. It was made of the finest cloth with handmade lace to cover it. I had a long train behind that was decorated with lace daisies. I was prepared for the unpredictable weather of New England and had a shawl made in case it would get cold. The shawl was lined with white fur and silk. These were the finest pieces of clothing I had ever owned. After my fitting, I hung them in my room and looked at them every night, counting down the days until my wedding.

Soon, it was the night before our wedding. After double checking that everything was ready, my family and my Elbert sat for dinner for my last evening as a single lady. Mother made a simple meal, as she had been preparing for tomorrow's wedding. Our modest celebration soon involved over one hundred people, all of whom were to gather under the tent Father had rented for the back garden. The four of us sat in silence, as we were all exhausted from the day of preparation.

Elbert excused himself, and I walked him to the door. We kissed and hugged; I wished him well, and he went off into the night. I had no interest in sleeping tonight. I was too excited, but Mother convinced me to have a cup of calming tea, then head to bed so I would be well rested for tomorrow. I tried with my might to calm down, but all I could think about was how tomorrow I would become Mrs. Elbert Monahan.

Chapter 20

I woke before the sun, eager for the special day to begin. I went to my bedroom door and discovered Mother had locked me in to make sure I would get a full night's rest. It was not time to get up yet. So I lay in bed staring at the ceiling, thinking of what my life was going to be like once I said yes.

He would be off on his journey while I took care of our home. I could cook what I wanted and have parties. I would start a book club and would not be at the mercy of my parents. When he would return, he would be mine. I would wake to his gentle kiss then head downstairs to prepare his breakfast. When he would return in the evening, I would take his hat, and he would give me another gentle kiss. At dinner, we would talk of our day's adventures, and at night, we would become one.

My eyes drifted over to my dress. I had high hopes my Elbert would return soon enough from his whaling adventure, bringing back the money we would need to start our new life in our own home. He had bragged just days before that he had one of the greatest crews he had ever assembled. He almost seemed more excited about his next ocean journey than about our wedding, but this was expected of a groom. I heard the chimes of the hall clock strike five. I needed my rest. I closed my eyes and forced myself back to sleep.

At seven o'clock, Mother entered my room with a tray of biscuits and tea. Behind her were Teresa and Maria. They had their dresses–baby blue to match the ribbons for my hair–and everything necessary to get me ready for my big day. Mother kissed me on the cheek and left, humming a cheerful tune. We chatted, sipped our tea, got into our dresses, and did our hair. As I was buttoned into my dress, I knew no matter how today went, I would end the day back in this house with my husband.

We descended the stairs. At the bottom stood Father, smiling. He took my arm, and we walked out the door to a waiting carriage and our driver. Father jokingly whispered, "You can still get out of this. I can have Peter take us to the pier, and we can grab the next boat out of here."

"I'm great, Father. I cannot wait to marry him!"

The carriage was decorated with dozens of flowers, a little surprise from Katherine. It was pulled by four of the most beautiful white horses I had ever seen. I heard they were a wedding gift from the Mayor, with whom Father was a long-time friend. The weather cooperated, and we were able to use an open carriage, making me feel like royalty. Father, Mother, and I climbed in, and my attendants Teresa, Maria, and Katherine followed in a second carriage. As we went through town, I imagined what all the people waving were thinking. When I was younger, seeing these carriages ignited dreams of my own wedding. I couldn't believe today was that day. The ride was a bit rough going over the cobblestones, but I did not care. As I waved back to everyone on the street, I felt like a queen on my way to marry my king.

We reached the church at ten past the hour. I looked around to see all the familiar faces. I could feel the warmth and love of those who showed up to see me. I knew this day would be one I would remember forever. I glanced at the groom's side and did not recognize many of the people there, but then again, we had not known each other that long. Where was Matthew? He was to be the best man, so I did not expect him to be around at this time, but I still hoped to see him. It would mean my Elbert would be near. I asked if we were all set to begin when it became half past the hour. Father lined up, and the music started. This day was already so perfect. The sun was shining, the church was splendid, and even my Elbert had arrived on time. I saw this as a great sign he could change.

As I walked down the aisle, Elbert was standing tall in his morning suit. He was a vision of strength and the most handsome man there. He was the only thing I could focus on. My dream of marrying him was coming true. Father kissed my hand and gave it to Elbert. Both of these men—who took a place in my heart—were smiling as much as I was.

The ceremony went off without incident. We pledged our love to each other and exchanged rings. We showed the world and God that we were a true couple and were committed to each other. As we walked out to cheers and the throwing of bird seed—I had read that rice was bad for birds and requested bird seed instead—I could see all the happy faces around me. It was surreal.

The whole congregation came back to our home with us. It was our home now. Mother had prepared the most impressive spread of food, and the cake was absolutely perfect. We cut a slice together, as was tradition, and spent the rest of the day in celebration. We had a local band and everyone joined in a dance. Teresa, Maria, and I held hands and spun around to the music, laughing. The large tent that was set up in our back yard covered all those whom Elbert and I counted as friends and family. The atmosphere was filled with companionship and love. That tent became a circus of my old and new life combining. A beautiful indication of my future. It was all that I had hoped for, and more. As the evening wound down, and our guests left, it was soon just me and my Elbert. There was no denying he was mine. He reached out for my hand, and we walked together inside our house for the first time as husband and wife.

That night, we sat in the parlor with Mother and Father, talking about the beauty of the day. "Everything looked beautiful, Zilla, and your dress was stunning," Mother said.

"The food was amazing!" added Father.

"We had great luck with the weather, and everyone seemed really happy!" I remarked.

Elbert smiled. When the clock struck nine o'clock, Father and Mother went to bed. My Elbert and I were finally alone, staring into each other's eyes. I did not want the moment to end. He took my hand, kissed it, and announced that he was going back to his ship since he had to leave very early in the morning. I pulled my hand away and dropped my glass. My whole life, I had been taught that waiting for the wedding night was important. This night was when we would truly become man and wife. This night, we were supposed to stay together as a couple and become one. Why did he want to leave? At that moment, my dreams seemed to shatter. Was this going to be our new life? Me at home, him off at sea or the tavern?

I had a glimmer of hope though as we walked to the door, and he asked if I would see him off in the morning to give us a last goodbye before departing for the next few months. I thought of the other wives I had seen over the years saying goodbye to their husbands. I would be one of them, and I would be strong. We kissed at the door, and I watched him disappear into the night.

I sunk into a chair in the parlor, exhausted from the day. I had had a vision of my wedding night ending with the two of us in bed together. Instead, I curled under the covers, alone.

Chapter 21

Katherine handed me a muffin as I slipped out the door and into the mist of the morning. I looked down at my ring and fiddled with it while I walked. I thought of the joy that had filled the previous day, and I thought of the dreams I had for my future, our future. As children, we created these ideas of what a life with our partner would be. Were mine fading like a ship leaving port? After spending last night alone, I wondered what exactly my future was to be.

I must have been walking fast because in what felt like no time, I arrived at the docks and found Elbert preparing to board his ship with his crew all bundled up and ready to go. Each man stood with their bags in hand, eager to embark on their next adventure. Other wives fussed over their husbands like they were their sons, making sure everything was in place. Children ran around with little concern that their fathers would be gone for a very long time. A mother wiped her departing son's dirty face with her spit as if he were still five years old. I caught Elbert's gaze and rushed over to see him. He picked me up in a large embrace, and we kissed. I was transported to another world as he spun me around and around. I returned to earth as he brought me back down. He called his crew to board, and I panicked. I was becoming a whaler's wife, one who was destined to wait and hope. I knew this was my lot when I fell for Elbert, but now it was a reality.

As the crew set off for sea, I waved from the pier and blew kisses until they faded into the horizon. When the ship could no longer be seen, I felt alone once again.

A woman approached me. "Would you like to come for dinner later in the week?"

I started to cry, and she put her arm on my shoulder and handed me a handkerchief to wipe my tears. I recognized the woman. She lived just down the road from me. I accepted the dinner invitation.

"I need to get the children ready for church, see you soon." She said goodbye.

I managed to smile and thank her.

On my way home, I tried to straighten up and calm myself, but I eventually collapsed on the street sobbing. Then I felt a hand on my shoulder. Matthew. He crouched right next to me and didn't say a word. He just sat beside me, comforting me. It felt nice not to be alone. Matthew offered to walk me home, and I accepted. We talked as old friends, and I let him know that although I was married yesterday, my happily ever after had not yet begun. I told him I was left all alone last night, and that I had to stay alone for the next few months. My life was not turning into what I expected. Was it a mistake marrying a whaler?

Matthew listened and reassured me. "Elbert will be home before you know it, and your love will conquer. Zilla, you are a strong, independent woman who can do anything."

I felt myself smiling, and in that moment, everything was alright. Later, at church, I ran into the woman from the docks and thanked her again for the invitation to dinner. Her name was Elizabeth and her husband James was the first mate, or number two, of *The Monahan*. This was his fifteenth sea voyage, and he was thrilled to join Elbert. They had three children; I often saw the two younger girls playing in the park by our street. I welcomed Elizabeth as a new friend and looked forward to spending an evening with an experienced whaler's wife. I hoped she would help me navigate my own voyage. And I hoped I could be a help to her as well.

Chapter 22

I arrived at Elizabeth's door with a basket of homemade biscuits. Two younger girls greeted me. They ushered me into the parlor where Elizabeth sat. The four of us snacked on the biscuits, chatted about the weather, and gossiped about the town. Soon their cook came in to announce dinner was served.

We sat around the table and were joined by the eldest child, John, who had just returned from his job at the local store. We said grace, passed around the food, and then the kids told me tales of their father's journeys. I felt at home with them, like I was being let into the society of whalers' families. Tonight, I sat and absorbed all that I could, noting that this family not only survived but thrived in this environment. It was at this gathering that I knew I could make it.

Elizabeth shared how having a good schedule helped with the lonely nights home without her husband. "I found having my own hobbies helps as well. I knit and garden, also having a good group of friends helps."

I thought to myself what my own schedule would look like. As I was still with my parents, it felt like not much would change, except now I wore a ring on my finger. It was great to hear what life was like for Elizabeth. After dinner, the girls rushed off to bed, and in the parlor, I spoke with John about his work and plans. He did not want to follow in his father's footsteps and have a life at sea; he wanted to be a lawyer. We coordinated for him to meet me at Matthew's office in the morning, where the two could speak of his career. Elizabeth appreciated this gesture, and I felt it cemented our friendship.

The next morning, I met John outside Matthew's office. At the reception desk, I greeted Maria, and she walked us to the back, where we found Matthew engulfed in his work. I knocked on his desk and asked if he had a moment for a friend. He smiled and stood up to hug me. I made introductions and soon, Matthew and John were discussing law school and his future goal of being a judge. John was enthusiastic in his answers; Matthew was impressed and offered him a chance to apprentice on the spot. He was to come two days a week to help in the office and learn more about the field. Matthew caught my glance and smiled, as I mouthed a thank you. They shook hands, and John excused himself, as he had to get to work.

Matthew asked if I could stay a few minutes and

closed the door. He wondered how I was doing. His concern was comforting to me, and I let him know I was staying busy and had found a new friend who was going through a similar experience. I invited Matthew to dine with my family later in the week, then took my leave.

Chapter 23

It had been about a month since Elbert left, and I had taken Elizabeth's advice on keeping to a schedule. It definitely staved off the loneliness. Each day had an agenda and a purpose. I started to feel like my life had changed in a positive way since walking down the aisle. My new routines had become my life, and I was enjoying them!

Mondays, I started off by accompanying Katherine to the market. We would catch up on the weekly gossip of the house and town, from who sat with whom at church the day before, to what Katherine heard about other families from her friends who worked for them. We would gather all the things Mother had written and then treat ourselves to a pastry for our walk home. I loved our little indulgences. Monday was like reliving my childhood with Katherine.

On Tuesdays, Pastor Smith's children came over for lessons. I enjoyed this day, as these boys were full of energy and enthusiasm for whatever I threw their way. With the weather warming up, we took it upon ourselves to explore the island. I brought them to the beaches to learn about shells and sea life, to the marshes to learn about tide pools, and to town, pointing out the different plants and flowers we saw along the way.

On Wednesdays, Elizabeth would come by for tea, and then we would head to the tavern together. She would share all the gossip from the other whalers' wives. At the tavern, Matthew and Maria would join, and the four of us would catch up. One time, Matthew and Maria came in with a story of a client who tried to pay Matthew in sardines. Though he accepted the payment, the whole office smelt like rotten fish for the rest of the day. Maria joked that it was so bad her eyes began to water, and John asked why she was crying.

On Thursdays, I met up with Elizabeth's girls after they got out of school for arts and craft. Each week, we worked on a new project. We canned vegetables, practiced embroidery, and went to the beach to paint the scenery with watercolors.

Fridays started to be one of my favorite evenings. Father had extended an open invitation to Matthew for dinner every week, which he accepted. So, each Friday, we would gather and discuss philosophy, history, scripture, anything academic. Father also enjoyed these nights having another person to debate with on things like the nature of religion and the classics. I did not always take part, but enjoyed listening and learning from them. Matthew's presence at these dinners helped grow our friendship, and I found myself looking forward to these evenings all week.

One morning, by request of my mother, I went to town to purchase a turkey for dinner. I took Katherine with me, as Mother wanted the kitchen to herself. When Katherine asked how I was managing without Elbert, I thought for a moment and realized I was doing well. I had found a community and purpose; I had found my own way outside my parents and my husband.

"Do you miss him?"

I again had to pause at this next question. I knew the answer I was supposed to give, but I had not really thought much about him over the past month. I had kept myself busy, and we had not yet had much time together as husband and wife. I gave the obligatory answer.

"He will be home before you know it." Katherine's words brought unease to my mind. I fiddled with my wedding ring, reminding myself that I was indeed married.

We returned home with the turkey, and Mother prepared it for the oven. I went about helping here and there. This Friday was a bit different. We had more guests coming. It was my one-month wedding anniversary, and since I was alone, Mother wanted to throw a special dinner to lift my spirits. I invited Elizabeth and John, Maria and Matthew, and Teresa and Michael. We added the leaf to the table and prepared a feast for all of us to share. This would be the first time Elizabeth would meet my other friends. It was going to be a dinner combining my old and new life. I was looking forward to it.

First to arrive and right on time was Matthew, along with Maria. As soon as I got them settled in the parlor with Father, there was another knock on the door. It was Elizabeth and John. I barely closed the door, and in came Teresa and Michael. We made our way to the parlor to join the others. Our group rounded out.

The men grouped together to talk business, and I introduced my oldest girlfriends to my newest girlfriend. Teresa sat on my left. She looked angelic in her yellow dress, which contrasted with her long brown hair. On my right was Elizabeth. She was a vision of sunshine with her golden hair flowing over her light blue frock. Across from me in our little circle was Maria. She had not changed from work and wore her secretary's brown dress with her hair perfectly pinned up. We started chatting about the gossip around town. Our conversations flowed as if the four of us had been friends for decades.

The biggest story on the island was that of a loose dog running around. Maria added her theory. "I think it's the Jones's dog."

Teresa shot down her sister's theory. "Their dog is black, and I heard the one that is running around is white."

Elizabeth piped in. "It is most definitely black and white. Mrs. White and I saw it sprinting down our street the other day."

This was the most exciting thing on Nantucket. I wondered what the whalers were seeing out at sea. Elizabeth regaled us with stories that her husband had told her of his fishing adventures. On one such journey, they were off the coast of Providence, Rhode Island, and they could see a school of fish swarming near their ship. The crew had lowered the net to catch as much of it as they could, but when they pulled up the net, all that was in there was a case of boots!

I looked around, ever the attentive host, to see how the men were doing. They seemed deep in conversation about something they felt a need to keep in a whisper. I returned to my girlfriends and asked Maria how John was working out.

She blushed. "He is a great asset to the office."

Elizabeth then shared with us how she ended up on the island. "I was taking care of my mother in Hudson, Massachusetts, which is a village of Marlborough, when one day at church I met James. It was love at first sight. We quickly married and after my mother passed, James suggested we move out to Nantucket so he would have a better chance of fulfilling his dream of being a whaler. We packed what we could, grabbed a spot on a ship to Nantucket, and never turned back. My mother left me some money, and we were able to hire a cook and a decent house for our growing family. When we moved here, I was expecting John, and now, with three little ones, I am glad we have the space."

Upon hearing his name, John came over, followed by Matthew and Michael.

I asked, "What was so important you three were discussing?"

Michael, dressed in a smart brown suit and the shortest of the three, giggled and looked at John, who was in a cream-colored suit coat and the tallest of the three. He also started giggling and looked at his new employer. Matthew, in an evening coat that contrasted with his blonde hair and blue eyes, piped up. "We were discussing the dog situation."

At this confession, all of us women burst into laughter. Mother came to let us know it was time to sit for dinner. We all stood and tried to stifle our giggles. I walked arm in arm with Maria to the dining room. At the table, Mother and I changed the seating chart to mix things up. We put the men on one side and the women on the other, with Mother and Father at the heads of the table. Mother had gone over the top for tonight's feast: a beef roast with rolls, potatoes, peas, carrots, and, of course, the catch of the day, haddock. We passed the serving plates, laughing and joking.

To add to our merriment, Father slipped when addressing Maria, calling her Teresa by mistake. It was a common occurrence, as they looked like twins, which they used to their advantage. Teresa answered for Maria and further confused Father. He commented, "Whichever one of you works for Matthew, whatever your name is: Teresa, Maria, George, Frank?"

"I'm actually known in the office as Maria Teresa Amelia, leader of the secretaries," Maria said.

Matthew choked on his wine. "I think I need to give you a raise, then."

Father finally got his question out, "Whoever you are, how is it working for these two clowns over here?"

"They are great and keep me on my toes, which makes the office even more fun."

We continued joking and enjoying the amazing meal Mother had prepared. After we had our fill, Mother informed us she made a special dessert that was set up in the parlor. So we shifted rooms and found freshly brewed coffee and small cakes. There was Victoria sponge, Battenberg, and a wonderful French treat of blancmange. I ran over to Mother and gave her a big hug, as blancmange was my favorite dessert.

I suggested we play charades. With the party in agreement, we split into teams. The game got very competitive. The highlight was watching Mother mimic a pastor, giving a great rendition of Father at the pulpit, including his drastic arm movements. The game went on for some time and only ended when the clock struck eleven and my friends needed to make their way home. They thanked us for a fantastic evening, and I walked them to the door. This evening reminded me I could survive anything. I had my friends and, with their help, I could make it through the lonely nights without my husband.

Chapter 24

Our weekly get-togethers as friends had become a common occurrence. Everyone took turns hosting, even Matthew. In May, he was eager to invite us over to indulge in his catch, as it was warm enough for him to go fishing, his favorite hobby. We ate his freshly caught fish, which he also prepared by himself. I was quite impressed with his cooking skills. Other times, our little crew would meet at The Pickled Quail for some drinks. These gatherings helped break up the loneliness of waiting for my Elbert.

June rolled around, and Elizabeth was the first to hear from the whalers. She had received a letter from her husband James informing her they were in Labrador, Newfoundland, a town on the coast of Canada. This meant they were on this side of the Atlantic and would be home by July. I impatiently waited for my letter to arrive, but it never came. Maybe it got lost, or he was too busy to write.

I focused on preparing for Elbert's return, since he

would be moving into our house. I had put off setting a space for him, as I did not know what he wanted. I enlisted Matthew to help me figure out what Elbert may want or need in our marital room. It was discussed with my parents that we would both move down the hall to the larger room. With his imminent return, I started moving my own things into it. Then Matthew and I met up in town to find the right furniture.

Elbert would need a small study, a shaving table, and a bureau for his clothes. We searched for something we thought he might like and settled on dark wood pieces that had nautical motifs. In time, I set up a small study in the room's corner with a bookcase and a leather chair for Elbert to read in. Next to the bed, I placed a shaving table, and I put his dresser right next to mine. I added little pieces to help the room seem more like a home.

I put out a decanter with some whiskey and laid it on a tray with two glasses. I imagined the two of us sipping it by the fire on a chilly night. On his bedside table, I arranged a small tray for his knick-knacks. I even took out my collection of sea glass and arranged it in a bowl so the sunlight could reflect its many colors. I added a table for his shaving accoutrements and found a beautiful brush set just for him.

I hung some nautical artwork as well. In town, I found a lovely painting of the sunset over the beach where we went on our first date. Its beauty, reflecting our personal connection, helped brighten the room. I also found a painting of a ship that looked very similar to *The Monahan*. I hoped it would bring some comfort to him, as he had lived on it for so long. It was beginning to feel like our home.

July came quickly. We heard on the fifth that our men were anchored off of Boston, waiting for fair seas and predicting to be back on the tenth. Elizabeth and I decided to organize a large picnic for all the families. We had little time to plan, but went in full force. Although I had never received a letter from Elbert, the tenth was soon upon us, and we would finally start our life as husband and wife.

Katherine, Mother, and Father helped me get the tables, chairs, and food to the greens in front of the church. Father had offered the space for our picnic, his way of giving back to the whaling community. We filled the carriage with supplies, and Peter drove us to the church. My crew was there to help: Matthew, Maria, John, Elizabeth, Teresa, and Michael. At noon, the families arrived. We gathered and chatted about what we had been up to the last few months. The wives shared the activities they were most looking forward to once their men returned home.

"I have a list a mile long of projects he needs to get done."

"It will be so nice having an extra set of hands."

Around one o'clock, the first sight of *The Monahan* on the horizon was spotted. The crowd cheered and made its way to the slip. About thirty minutes later, the ship docked and dropped anchor. I waited with impatience for Elbert to come off the ship. Elizabeth was standing next to me the whole time and kept reminding me that our husbands would be the last off. She regaled me with a story of her first time welcoming James home. "I was so excited I ran as fast as I could toward the ship, slipped, and fell, skirt above my head. I was laughing so hard that I almost missed James!" She held my hand, as I was shaking in anticipation.

Finally, James and my Elbert disembarked the ship. I sprinted toward him, no longer wanting to wait another moment away from him. As he walked up the pier, we met, and he dropped his bag. He wrapped his brawny arms around me, and I embraced him back. For a moment, it was just the two of us. Time stood still. Then he picked up his bag, grabbed my hand tight, and we walked together as a married couple for the first time since our wedding all those months ago.

The picnic began with tales of adventures from both the whalers and their wives. The men spoke of the weather and their time on the ship. "Bob thought he was great at cards, but in comes John, and he cleaned us out!"

The wives brought the men up on the gossip around town. "This dog was getting into all the gardens!"

"I heard it was Mr. Thurston's."

Elbert turned to me during the feast to thank me for helping to organize a celebration for the families. "I'm glad I can count on you to keep things going at home." He was satisfied that I had taken to my role as captain's wife so well. I felt great pride.

As the afternoon turned into evening, families made their way back home, and some men headed to the tavern. Soon it was just Father, Mother, Elbert, me and the church's women's group who had volunteered to help clean up. I wanted to help, but Mother turned me down, and Father urged Elbert and me to take his carriage back home. Elbert and I agreed to leave but decided to walk in the wonderful summer weather.

I could barely hold in my excitement. I almost tripped a few times on the cobblestone, as I was so lost in his presence that I had forgotten to look where I was going. Elbert was so busy during the picnic, but now we had a moment for him to share his personal stories of the journey. He told me the great news that they had caught a whale as big as the last time. I pulled him in for an embrace, but he seemed distant. I shrugged it off, as today had been a hectic day. I squeezed his hand tight to show him I was there.

"I am sorry, I am exhausted after the journey. I am looking forward to getting home and settled."

Soon we were at the front door. I stopped before entering, hoping we would fulfill one of my dreams of when a new husband carries his wife over the threshold for good luck. Elbert hesitated and gave me a stare as to why I was just standing there. I cleared my throat. He figured out what I was indicating, and with a sigh, he lifted me over the threshold and put me down on the other side. Once inside, I grabbed Elbert's hand and led him up the stairs. "I have a surprise for you!" He lugged behind me down the hall to our room. I couldn't wait to see his reaction. "Close your eyes, it's a surprise!"

Elbert grunted and closed his eyes.

"Okay, one, two, three, and open!"

"Oh, it's…it's fine."

"What is wrong? I tried to think what you may like and need here." I pointed out the small study I made, the shaving table, and all the little details.

Elbert went straight to the decanters and found a glass. "Which one is whiskey?"

I pointed. He poured himself a glass and slumped into the leather chair. I tried to sit with him.

"I am tired. Please leave me alone for a while."

I spun away and on my way out, I said, "Just remember, we dress for seven here, so please be in the parlor by then." With that, I closed the door.

I went down the stairs with heavy steps to the kitchen. Katherine was hard at work on dinner. "I was not expecting you!" she said.

We had talked many times about what I was hoping for once my husband was home. It did not include helping with dinner preparation the night he returned. I asked for a task, and she handed me a bowl of carrots to peel. I filled Katherine in on the picnic and our walk home. I explained he was now upstairs resting, as he was very tired from the trip.

Suddenly, we heard a loud noise coming from above, like furniture moving. We looked at each other. There was no explanation I could provide, so we just looked at each other in silence.

Mother soon returned from the picnic. She was as shocked as Katherine to see me working in the kitchen. I explained Elbert was tired. We heard another loud noise coming from our room. "Sure…resting…" Mother quipped.

The three of us prepared dinner in silence that night. When it was close to seven o'clock, I went upstairs to make sure Elbert was getting ready. I entered the room, and he scurried away from the bookcase. I reminded him we were to meet downstairs in about five minutes. He grunted. I grabbed my shawl and left the room.

In the parlor, Father offered me a sherry, which I gladly accepted. Mother joined, and the three of us sat and chatted, all the while taking turns checking the clock. When Elbert arrive, it was half past the hour, and he almost knocked over Katherine as she was coming to let us know that dinner was served. We walked into the dining room, and there was an air of tension. It was a new thing, us being two couples. Father looked as if he wanted to call Elbert out for being late, but Mother loudly asked Elbert if he would like any potatoes. The rest of dinner was one of silence.

After eating, we returned to the parlor for a drink. I was quite exhausted and excused myself, hoping Elbert would join me. Instead, he excused himself to the tavern. Not wanting to rock the boat, I bid him goodbye and went upstairs alone. I changed into my night clothes and sunk into our bed. As I laid there, I imagined my Elbert next to me, holding me close, and I fell asleep.

I awoke around midnight when he returned from the tavern. He stumbled into bed, smelling of whiskey and smoke. I asked how his evening was, and he hushed me, beckoning me to go back to sleep. I closed my eyes again and heard him tinker around near the books. Then I drifted back to sleep.

Chapter 25

I awoke to the sun shining and the birds chirping. I rolled over and found that Elbert was not in bed with me. Maybe he was an early riser and had already gone downstairs. I was mistaken. There he was, asleep in the chair by the bookcase. He was still in his clothes from the night before, snoring.

I decided to let him sleep and went downstairs for breakfast, where Katherine and Mother were already enjoying a cup of tea. They were chatting while waiting for the muffins to bake. "It was midnight when he returned," said Katherine.

Upon seeing me, they jumped a bit and apologized for gossiping about my husband. Within minutes of setting up breakfast, Father arrived, and Mother poured him a cup of tea. I snuck upstairs to find Elbert unpacking his bag. When he noticed me, he started shoving things back in. I told him breakfast was ready. "Please come down and join."

"Mhmm," he grunted.

At the bottom of the stairs, I paused for a moment. My Elbert and I were supposed to be together, cheerfully getting to know each other. We were supposed to go to bed together and wake up next to each other. He was supposed to answer me in words, not grunts. This was not what I had imagined. Perhaps he was still tired from his journey. Surely things would improve.

We had finished our breakfast when Elbert walked in. I offered to sit with him while he ate, but he seemed perturbed. Was he upset I did not wait for him to eat?

Once my parents left, Elbert spoke. "A wife should stay up for her husband. Why were you already in bed? And it was very rude of you to not wait for me this morning. You are my wife, I should be your priority, not your parents."

I apologized. "This is all new to me. I did not know how long I would have to wait, so I did not know if waiting was possible."

He shrugged off my apology, and I promised to do better. We changed the subject to our plans for the day. He was going to the pier to work on ship maintenance. I asked if we should meet for lunch in town and offered to pack a basket for us. He declined, not knowing if he could take a break; he would bring a sandwich.

Elbert got up from the table and kissed me on the forehead. I grabbed our dirty plates and followed him downstairs to the kitchen. I heard him speaking to

Katherine, demanding her to make him a sandwich for lunch and to be quick about it. I was about to step in, but Katherine shot him right back, "Sit down and wait, sir, I don't work for you. I work for Reverend Harper."

I piped in to keep the peace and offered to make it. Elbert thanked me and gave Katherine a look of disgust. I sent him upstairs to get ready for the day and told him his lunch would be ready by the time he was. He huffed off to the stairs as I grabbed the bread. Katherine gave me the look, the look that meant I was in trouble. Before she could say anything, I told her I knew the way he talked to her was wrong, and I would speak to him about it. I knew she no longer had any respect for him.

On the way upstairs, I heard Elbert having cross words with Peter. "I hear you're the driver," he said. "I need you to be ready every morning at nine to take me to the pier. You do not expect me, one of the men of the house, to walk now, do you?"

When I saw Peter, he looked nervous and tried to come up with an answer. I cleared my throat and stepped in. "Peter, would you mind taking Elbert into town today? I know you are driving Father to church. Maybe you could drop him off along the way?"

Elbert scowled. "I will just walk, but tomorrow you better be ready." He pointed aggressively at Peter's face.

I mouthed a sorry to Peter and turned my cheek to Elbert for a kiss. He went on his way, and I was left there in disappointment. I tried to explain to Peter that he did not need to worry. He was not obligated to drive to town every day, and I would talk to Elbert about it.

When Ebert left, I found myself free for the rest of the morning. I went to Father's study to see if there was anything he needed help with. He had me sit. "Are you happy, dear Zilla?"

"Of course I am. My husband is home. What a silly question."

Father cleared his throat, which meant he did not believe me.

"I am learning how to be happy with Elbert."

"Elbert was out very late last night."

I acted dumbfounded, and Father gave me his look; he did not believe me again. "Yes, I noticed it was late."

"If he is going to be home so late, please ask him to come through the backdoor so as not to disturb the others in the house."

I agreed to pass on the message.

"Is everything alright?"

I answered in the affirmative. "Will that be all, Father?" I was sent on my way.

Next, I went to see if Mother needed anything. I walked downstairs into the kitchen, where she and Katherine were talking about Elbert's outburst. I cleared my throat to let them know I had entered the room. They apologized half-heartedly for speaking once again about my husband. I asked if there was anything with which I could help. Mother asked if it was possible for me to do the shopping. I accepted the task.

On my way to the market, I ran into Elizabeth, and we walked together into town. I questioned her about her husband's behavior after arriving back home. She blushed, giggled, and answered that they reconnected all night, and he was in high spirits. I confessed to her I had gone to bed on my own and found Elbert asleep in the chair in the morning. She tried to reassure me he must have just been too tired and needed to rest. I took her into my confidence. "We have yet to share the same bed."

Elizabeth gasped. The look of shock was quite visible on her face. I tried to explain, "He left the morning after our wedding, and we are living with my parents now." She thought this was odd and wanted to know about any other odd behavior. I let her know about how he spoke to Katherine this morning. She was appalled, then tried to justify it, but then just apologized for it all. She took my arm and comforted me along our walk, which had turned into a very silent walk.

We stopped for lunch, and Elizabeth wanted to know what was next for my marriage and to share her ideas on how to improve it. We sat at a quiet table in the corner of the teahouse. They were known for their wonderful lunches and quiet atmosphere. Once our food arrived, Elizabeth asked, "How long are the two of you staying with your parents?"

"Permanently, according to him."

That shocked look returned to Elizabeth's face. "He just needs to learn that he isn't the captain of the home, just his ship." She reassured me he most likely only thought of what he was doing during whaling season, and had forgotten that there were two in a relationship.

"Does this explain how he spoke to Katherine this morning?"

She assured me that Katherine would put him in his place, and he would adjust to the new living situation. We chatted about making a plan for Elbert and me to connect and share a bed tonight. We finished our meals, and I suggested we finish the shopping and walk home by the pier, hoping to run into Elbert. Along the pier, I saw his ship and a figure climbing out from the deck below. I waved, but the person did not wave back.

That evening, I greeted Elbert at the door with a kiss and an offer to take his hat. He obliged, and I let him know dinner would be on the table soon. He snapped, "I will come to dinner when I am ready."

Father saved me from snapping back at him. "Elbert, dinner is in ten minutes, and if you want to join us, you need to change, otherwise you can find food elsewhere."

Nine minutes later, Elbert walked into the dining room in a clean shirt and his hair presentable. We sat and had a cordial meal. After dinner, we retired to the parlor and on the way, I pulled Elbert aside. "About Peter, he already has such a busy schedule, he cannot take you into town every day. If you would like, I could walk with you!"

Elbert grunted.

"Are you going to the tavern this evening?"

He said he was thinking of it. I tried to be coy, as Elizabeth had suggested. "There is something special waiting for you upstairs when you return." I hoped my wink and smile resonated with him. He smiled back, kissed my cheek, and walked me into the parlor. Not five minutes later, he announced he was on his way out. He looked for the bell to ring for Katherine. When he could not find it, he went to the hall and started yelling her name. I got up from my chair and stood at the door, curious to see what all the fuss was about.

"Yes?" Katherine said as she entered the hall.

"When I call for you, I expect you to come!"

Katherine gritted her teeth and half-smiled. "What is it you wanted?"

"I am going out. Where did you happen to leave my hat this time?"

Katherine was holding her tongue. I was about to intervene, but Mother stopped me, as she felt Katherine had it handled.

"Your hat is where it belongs, on the hat rack by the door. Will there be anything else? If not, I must return to my duties."

Elbert brought up his fist, then dropped it. He snatched his hat and snarled on his way out.

Father shot me a look. I had to instruct my husband to use the back entrance when he returned. I spoke up. Elbert agreed and left.

I excused myself to prepare for his return tonight. I prettied myself, adding powder to my face and bosom. I unpinned my hair and let it flow. I had bought lipstick in town with Elizabeth and applied it to my lips. I looked in the mirror and smiled. I took a deep breath and put on my thinnest nightgown, hoping it would be the most enticing to him. I got under the covers, opened my book, and waited. The candle next to my bed burned bright, and I watched the door, waiting for my Elbert to walk in.

The candle burned lower, and I had a hard time keeping my eyes open. I looked at the clock on the wall. It was eleven o'clock. I would give him five more minutes, then I was going to blow out my candle and retire for the night. I watched each second tick by. At five past eleven, I figured he would not be back before I fell asleep. I leaned over to blow out the candle, and I heard the door creek open. I sat back up in bed. "Who's there?"

Elbert shushed me and told me to go back to bed.

"I am awake. I am waiting for you."

He undressed and joined me in bed. For the first time in our six months of marriage, we lay together as husband and wife.

Chapter 26

I awoke a new woman. I felt more connected to Elbert than I had anyone else in my life. The night before, we had become one, and for a moment, it was just us in the world and everything was perfect. The sun was glowing, and the birds were singing to me. I rolled over to find my Elbert already gone.

I walked into the dining room and saw Mother and Father enjoying their breakfast, but no Elbert. I sat, still smiling from the night before, but a bit worried about where he was. I asked what plans my parents had for the day, then asked the question I feared the answer to: "Where is Elbert?"

My mother explained that he had been down earlier but needed to head to his ship to do some work. I played it off, lying that I had forgotten. I had no idea what he was up to. I knew little of what he actually did, but after last night, I thought I was his priority, at least until morning. I decided to make a surprise trip to see him on his ship. It was my prerogative as a wife to drop in from time to time, and after last night, I thought it was time to have a romantic run-in.

In the kitchen, I asked Katherine to pack a basket for us, then I went upstairs to put on my blue dress that brought out my eyes and, as many said, the warmth of my smile, which I considered my best feature. I stopped in the garden and picked a fresh daisy for my hair. I walked along the road in my own world, fantasizing of all the things we would speak of during my surprise visit. In my mind, I would go to the dock, knock on the side of his ship, and call out to him, "Elbert, sweetheart?" Then he would run up the steps from below, grab me in his arms, and we would take our picnic to the beach.

The clock struck noon as I walked to the end of the dock and yelled out his name. I tried again, this time knocking on the side of the ship. I asked permission to come on board, hoping the ceremonious term would get his attention. I heard no reply and was about to give up when I saw him walking toward his ship. I called out to him, and he stopped. "What are you doing here?"

Suddenly, I felt guilty for disturbing him. Was I out of line? I apologized and spent the next five minutes explaining myself. He sent me away with a full basket and a pit in my stomach. Why was he being so distant and secretive? He seemed to be hiding something from me. Something wasn't right. I thought about what I was doing wrong. What I had done wrong the night before. I thought our love was strong, and that he would want to spend time with me but always seemed upset.

I shook off the encounter and decided to share my basket with Elizabeth. As I knocked on her door, I felt the urge to hide what had just happened between Elbert and me. She did not need to know I had made a fool of myself trying to surprise him. Elizabeth answered, and I held up my basket. "Would you like to join?"

She hesitated. "I was just on my way out to Teresa's house for lunch."

"Oh, never mind. I'll be on my way then."

Elizabeth noticed the stress in my voice. "Why don't you join us? We wouldn't want that basket to go to waste."

I agreed, and the two of us walked in silence to Teresa's house. I was too scared to talk about what had happened, and Elizabeth was too scared to ask. We sat in Teresa's garden with a plethora of food and chatted about this and that, and soon the question I was dreading came up. My two friends wanted to know why I had a basket ready to go. I stuttered, not wanting to tell the whole truth. "It was meant for Elbert and me, but he was busy."

Teresa gave a knowing look, one that I knew well: She only partly bought my story, but she would not pry until I was ready. She focused on what had happened last night. I giggled and blushed, and Teresa knew I had connected with Elbert for the first time. They wanted details, and I gave them the whole story. Well, close enough to the truth, I just left out the part where he came home after drinking and was gone before I woke up in the morning.

We talked about our husbands, the romantic and annoying things they did, and I tried to only talk of the positives. While their grievances were small things like not picking up socks or leaving drinks on the table without a coaster, mine were much greater issues. So I made up small examples, like he butters his toast in such a way that it makes far too many crumbs.

When Teresa's children returned from school, we said our goodbyes. I felt dread on my way back home. I did not know what version of Elbert would show up. I found my mother where she usually was this time of day, in the kitchen, busy preparing dinner. I asked if we could talk. She agreed if I peeled the potatoes. I grabbed a potato and asked, "What can I do to be a great wife to Elbert?"

Mother stopped stuffing the duck. She looked at me. It meant: You know the answer to that question, young lady, but I shall answer it. She told me to anticipate his needs, try to have his favorite treats in a dish in our room and his favorite liquor always stalked.

"What about taking time together, just the two of us?"

She told me not to plan such things until I knew exactly what time he had available. She told me it took a lot to learn about a man, which usually happened during courting, but since we skipped much of that, I had to do it now. She suggested that she and Father would go to town one evening, leaving us to have an intimate evening at home. I agreed, and we planned to talk about this with our husbands at dinner. Mother put her hand on my shoulder and reassured me it was going to be alright. I felt comforted. We prepared the rest of the meal together in silence.

At dinner, Mother breached the subject of her and Father taking an evening in town. There was a band playing in the park Saturday, and she suggested the two of them should go. I encouraged them to take the night out, that they deserved it. Elbert barely looked up from his plate of food until called on for his opinion. He grunted in approval of the plan.

"You and I can have a quiet evening at home!" I exclaimed.

He grunted again and excused himself.

I helped clean up the table, and Elbert left for the tavern. Mother encouraged me to follow him, but I didn't want to surprise him again and feel that embarrassment. But Mother urged me to go and even suggested I invite my friends. I kissed her on the cheek and ran out the door. When I arrived, Matthew and Maria were there. We found an open table in the corner, and Matthew went to the bar to get our drinks. Maria asked how married life was treating me.

I answered with only positives, since that was what people wanted to hear. "Things are fine! I found a new little ship that looks like Elbert's for his bedside table." I asked how the law office was doing.

She followed suit with her own positives. "Everything is good, business is steady, and John and Matthew are great to work with!"

Matthew returned and informed me that my husband was at the bar. I acknowledged this and let Matthew know we came separately, and Elbert may join us later. I felt that dread again in my stomach. Had I gone too far coming to the tavern tonight? I started to question everything and barely participated in the conversation with my friends. I felt I needed an explanation for my presence here, and that was all I could focus on.

I scanned the bar area and found Elbert; he was speaking to a woman. She looked slightly older than me, wearing a beautiful green dress with her curly black hair bouncing around her shoulders. I kept my eye on them the whole time, missing much of the conversation at our table. It took Matthew clearing his throat for me to realize he had asked me a question. "What was it you asked? Sorry, I was in another world." He wondered what had taken me out of the world. "Elbert is speaking to another woman over there, whom I do not know." Matthew looked bothered.

Maria spoke up, "You are newlyweds still trying to figure out things, and he may have forgotten to tell you."

I nodded in agreement but still kept an eye on Elbert and his companion. When we decided to call it a night, I grabbed my shawl and left Elbert deep in conversation with the mystery woman.

Maria locked arms with me and leaned in close. "How are you doing?"

I smiled and answered fine, just as I had when her sister Teresa asked.

"I'm here, as is my whole family, if you ever want to talk."

I thanked her and changed the subject, asking what was going on with her and Matthew.

She smiled. "Nothing romantic. He is acting as my chaperone so I can meet a man at the tavern like you did."

Hearing this warmed my heart.

"My mother would never let me be seen out without someone respectable, and my boss fits the ticket."

Matthew was a rock for those around him, always putting others' needs first. He had made his mark on the island already, offering free services for those in need and always having an open ear to whomever needed it. When the school was threatened by their landlord, Matthew stepped in and helped them rewrite their lease so that there would always be a school on the island. I liked that about him. He was a great friend, someone anyone could rely on. Maria and I arrived at my home. I thanked her again for a great evening and walked around the back to the kitchen entrance to not disturb my parents. I took off my shawl and sat at the table.

I let out a sigh of relief; I could be asleep before Elbert was home. I was in no mood to argue with him or be lectured by him. As I got under the covers, I heard him come in the front door. Why had he not used the back entrance? I closed my eyes, pretending to be asleep, as he scurried like a mouse into the room. I lifted my head, ever so slightly, and thought I saw him putting something inside a book. He spun around, as if he knew I was watching, and I closed my eyes, feigning sleep. When I dared to look again, his hands were empty. I lay there frozen as he went back out the door. This was the first of many nights he wouldn't spend in our house.

Chapter 27

I awoke to rain, one of those gray days that the island was known for. The weather matched my mood. I had spent an evening alone. My husband did not even acknowledge me, or even kiss my forehead before scurrying out of the room like a rat, never to return until the following day. And now I had proof that he was indeed hiding things from me. I needed to know who that woman was, and what I saw last night. I went downstairs, focused on tomorrow night's dinner and determined to get to know my husband better.

In the kitchen, I asked Katherine what I should prepare for Elbert. She handed me a cup of tea and told me to sit down for breakfast first. I finished eating a muffin and asked again. She suggested a beef roast with potatoes and carrots and a blueberry pie for dessert. My mouth watered. I started a list of what I would need to buy in town. On my way out, Father stopped me. He was going into town as well and offered to take me with him.

In the carriage, Father asked how I was doing, and I answered with the usual answer, "I'm fine." He wanted to know if I could speak to Elbert about his behavior around the house. I acted puzzled even though I knew Father was talking about him coming in at all hours, letting no one know where he was going, and how he talked to Katherine and Peter. I told Father I would address these issues, also noting that Elbert was a captain and sometimes forgot he wasn't the captain of our home. Father gave me the look that meant: You know the simple solution; move out. We both knew it, but neither of us would say it.

Father dropped me at the market and promised to be back in a half hour to pick me up. I thanked him for the ride and went about my shopping. I got the finest cut of beef from the butcher and found beautiful potatoes and carrots. The baker had a blueberry pie that looked absolutely delicious. I ran into Leonard, a whaler friend from childhood, and asked him about Elbert.

"Elbert Monahan? Well, all of us whalers know not to get hired on his crew. He is cruel to his men."

I dismissed this answer. Elbert was a strong captain, and maybe Leonard did not want to do the hard work. But then again, when I had asked the harbormaster about Elbert, he said, "That man...he is one of my biggest problems. You know he lives on his ship and complains about every little thing, and he never pays his docking fees on time."

It seemed that no matter who I talked to, they all had a negative thing to say about Elbert. The grocer complained that he demanded things and never paid his tab. Mr Jones at The Pickled Quail quipped that when Elbert came in, he knew that there would be a lot more to clean up. Apparently, Elbert tended to throw his glass when he got cut off due to being a disturbance. Surely all this bravado was a mask. He felt the need to act this way to gain respect from those around him, to better establish himself on our island. It made me think: Had I simply accepted his issues in order to keep the sanity in our relationship? Was I ignoring his bad behavior because, in my mind, love could triumph over all?

With my shopping list fulfilled, including a special bottle of wine, I went to the meeting spot, and like clockwork, Father arrived exactly on time. We rode home in the gray of the day, talking about what Mother would prepare for lunch, and joking about the absurd amount of things Mother seemed to make these days. Maybe she was fattening up Elbert for her secret stew recipe.

When we arrived home, Father stopped me before leaving the carriage. He held my hand. "Zilla, no matter what, your mother and I are always here for you."

I smiled and squeezed his hand. "Thank you, Father, I am fine, just a few bumps in the road as I learn how to be a wife."

I went down the stairs into the kitchen to find Katherine at the stove, and Elbert sitting at the table with a knife and a piece of wood, whittling. I said hello to Katherine and kissed Elbert on the cheek.

He said, "Where were you? And why didn't you tell me first?"

I apologized and explained it happened quickly as Father was on his way to town, so I was able to catch a ride with him.

"Tell me, what is in that basket? What did you purchase?"

I said it was dinner for us tomorrow, wanting to keep the specifics a surprise. He looked confused. I reminded him that my parents were going to a concert, and that I had a special evening planned for just the two of us. He grunted. I kissed his cheek again and winked. I would make it an evening he would not forget. He half smiled and wandered out of the room.

Katherine let out an audible sigh of relief. "Your husband is insufferable." She was whisking some cream, and her anger showed as she whisked faster and faster until the cream spilled out. "He sat there with his knife for the past hour staring as I worked. I was terrified that he was going to use the knife on me, and I grabbed one myself." She pulled a small paring knife out of her apron pocket. "He did not speak except to ask, every few minutes, when you would be back." Katherine started shaking the knife at me. "He seemed angrier and angrier every time I answered I did not know, again and again."

I apologized for his behavior. It seemed everyone in the house was on eggshells around him. I knocked on the door to Father's study, and he welcomed me in. I sat and asked what I should do about Elbert and his attitude around the home. Father suggested I investigate getting our own place. I knew this would be the right solution, but how would I approach the subject with Elbert? It was his idea that we stay in the house. How could I convince him to move out and into a small place, just the two of us? Father went to his bookshelf and took out an account book I had seen before but had never seen open. He explained he had put aside money for a house for my future family, and in this book, I could see how much money I had for a new place.

I looked at the number. There was enough for Elbert and me to live comfortably in a little house by the pier, close enough that he could always be near his ship. I hugged Father and thanked him. He helped me come up with a plan to tell Elbert, and I decided I would bring it up at our romantic dinner the following night. I was excited at the prospect of starting my life with Elbert in our own place. All our issues would be resolved.

That night would be like every other night since Elbert had returned home from sea: We ate as a family, and then he went to the tavern. I knew this routine, so I invited Matthew and Maria to play cards after dinner, hoping

Elbert would change his plans and stay with us, but alas, he was off. I assumed he was meeting that woman.

I told Matthew and Maria about my plan to move out and get a place for Elbert and me. They both were excited but wondered how Elbert would react to my family providing the home for us. We played cards late into the night, talking about what type of place I should get. Maria said I should have a place with many bedrooms for our growing family.

I let out a deep sigh. "Well…" I paused, searching for the right way to tell my friends. "Elbert does not want children, and it is his idea we should live with my parents."

Maria asked, "For the short term, because he left after the wedding?"

I looked at my cards. "Well, no, it's permanent as of right now. He doesn't want to live anywhere else."

Matthew and Maria looked at each other and then at me. Matthew spoke up. "He sounds controlling. What other parts of your life does he control?"

I paused again to think about it and disregarded the question. "It does not matter much. I barely see him anyway. He heads to The Pickled Quail every night and when he gets home, he tends to sleep in his leather chair."

The expressions on my friends said it all. This was not normal, and my situation needed to change. Matthew interjected, "I see him with a woman every time I am at the tavern. It doesn't look like a love connection, maybe a friend."

I let them know I had no idea who she was and why they met every night. I felt comfortable enough to tell Maria and Matthew that Elbert was hiding something from me. "It was dark, but I swear I saw him fiddling with a book in our room last night."

I do not know if it was the drinks or the prospect of a mystery, but Matthew declared we had to snoop in that bookshelf and find out what he was hiding. I knew it was not the right move, but I agreed. The three of us went upstairs, determined to discover Elbert's secret.

Chapter 28

We stood in the doorway, and I pointed at the bookshelf. We each started pulling books out at random, flipping through them, hoping that one would hold the secret. Page after page after page, but nothing seemed out of the ordinary. Then, Matthew opened a book of poems where the pages had been cut out and a hidey-hole was filled with gold coins.

Where did they come from? Why were they hidden? I was furious. Marriage was about honesty and transparency. It had me thinking that there was more. I paced up and down the floor until Maria raised her hand and said, "Keep walking, but slower. I hear something."

As I took a few more steps, we all heard the change in sound over one part of the rug. I knelt, lifted the rug, and Matthew handed me a knife to pry up the loose board. I could not believe my eyes. The hole was filled with jewelry and gems. There were pearl necklaces, ruby rings, and diamond bracelets. Maria, Matthew, and I sat there in shock, wondering what to do next.

We placed everything back as it was, ran down the stairs, and slunk into chairs in the parlor. I was shaking. Perhaps it was his family heirlooms that he was hiding? Matthew and Maria had other ideas; they wanted to know more about his latest trip to sea. Elbert had told me it was a success, but didn't share any other details. He hadn't even written to me while away. All I knew of the trip came from Elizabeth and her husband, who had said they stopped in Newfoundland to sell their catch.

Matthew speculated Elbert wasn't a fisherman, but a smuggler. I dismissed this notion; the first time we met he talked about catching the biggest whale. I paused and reflected on Elbert's mysterious ways. He was always secretive about how he came upon his wealth and never spoke of what happened on his trip. In fact, he had always been secretive about everything. From our first meeting, he didn't even share his own name. He lied or hid things about his past, like owning his own ship and having a steady crew.

The more I thought about it, the more I realized our entire relationship was him keeping his secrets and me trying to pry them out of him. I felt like I was back to day one with him, just knowing his name and not much else. The clock struck eleven. It was getting late. I thanked my friends and bid them goodnight, locked the door, and headed up to bed. I sat awake, rethinking every interaction with Elbert.

The next morning, I awoke alone, more alone than any other morning. I entered the dining room to find Mother and Father drinking tea, but no Elbert. We lingered over breakfast as my parents talked about tonight's concert. I smiled, delighted by their love and desire to spend time with each other. Then the dread crept back into my stomach. After what I had discovered last night, I was no longer eager for the romantic evening I had planned with Elbert. I felt anxious. I needed to get more answers, and I knew who to go to: Elizabeth.

I jotted an urgent message and asked Peter to bring it to her immediately. He obliged and was on his way. I finished my breakfast and took my dirty dishes down to the kitchen.

Later in the day, Peter returned with an answer. Elizabeth said she would be over as soon as the girls were off to their friend's house in about an hour.

Katherine asked me what was happening. I kept the secret from her, stating that Elizabeth was coming over to help me get ready for my special dinner. Katherine turned the sink faucet off and handed me a note in which she had outlined everything I needed to do for my evening with Elbert. "I am off the rest of the day and will be back at work on Monday." Then she threw me a towel, and I joined her at the sink to dry the dishes.

"I hope you have a wonderful break. By the way,

have you seen my husband?"

"Elbert?"

"Yes, I'm pretty sure I just have the one."

"I have not seen him... But I was not particularly looking for him."

We both giggled and got back to the task at hand. When we finished cleaning the dishes, she asked me to sit. I was nervous about what she was about to say.

"You have always been like a daughter to me, and I do not like to see you upset. I notice you are on edge whenever Elbert is around." She grabbed my hands. "Please don't lose the happy part of yourself. I am always here for you whenever you need to talk."

I thanked her and eased her mind. I would be fine, and she could enjoy her time off. After Katherine left, I sat at the kitchen table thinking about the past few days, how all those close to me had had the same conversation with me. After last night's revelations, I realized they must have seen something in Elbert that I had not. I was grateful for all the support I had from my family and friends, and I felt confident about tonight's dinner. It was time I figured out exactly who I married.

Finally, Elizabeth arrived. I handed her carrots, and she went about peeling and slicing them. "Zilla, please tell me, what is going on?"

I took a deep breath and asked what stories James had told her about the latest sea voyage. She acted confused, like I should know what our men were up to. I asked a more poignant question: "Do you know exactly what happened on their voyage? Elbert shares very little, and I am at a loss." Then I revealed what Matthew, Maria, and I found upstairs.

Elizabeth turned white. I knew she was keeping something from me and pressed her for more information.

"I don't know, not for certain. James returned with a bag of coins but never explained what they had done at sea, only that he didn't have to come home anymore smelling of whale…"

We went through every interaction we had with our husbands since they had been home to come up with a picture of where all this treasure had come from. We decided to bring in James, knowing he was the one who could answer our questions. Elizabeth sent word to him through Peter, and soon James was sitting in my kitchen.

Chapter 29

We stared at each other and waited for someone to break the silence. James sat on one side of the table, Elizabeth and I on the other side. He spoke first. "Why am I here?"

I looked at Elizabeth, and she nodded, assuring James that he was in no trouble, sounding like a mother, not his wife. Her tone was calm but stern; she was blunt, asking what he had been up to on his sea journey. James stuttered and stalled. I piped in, "We really need to know."

He started out saying that he was hired by the captain, thinking it was a whaling ship. I gave him an accusatory look. How could he not know what the ship's mission was after being hired? He assured us he did not know, not until the second day at sea when he saw a whale and called out to Elbert that the crew should ready a boat to harpoon the creature, exclaiming how lucky they were to see one so quickly. "The Captain rejected my claim of a whale sighting and said we were to continue east toward Ireland. I was confused, but I followed his orders. It wasn't until we arrived in Ireland that I realized what we were actually doing: smuggling whiskey from Ireland to Newfoundland. At that point, I had no choice but to keep going and follow along with his plan. I was weeks away from home." James described Elbert had a temper and lashed out at those who questioned him.

"Did the others know this was a smuggling trip? Or did my husband trick everyone?"

"My sense was that some had an idea of what was going on, but no one knew the extent of it until we docked in Ireland."

I thanked James for being honest with us. My heart was beating fast. Who did I marry? Was he really from Ireland? Did he actually run away from heading his family clan? I asked James why he didn't speak up until now? He explained he had thought I was in on the business and figured I had already told Elizabeth.

James stood. "Be careful around the captain. He is a man with a temper who should not be trusted." He hugged Elizabeth and left.

Since Matthew and Maria knew about the treasure, and I trusted their judgement, I suggested they come help me and Elizabeth come up with a plan. I asked Peter to send a note to Matthew, with a promise of a slice of pie, and that this was the last note he would have to deliver today. Peter smiled and thanked me for giving him a chance to get out of the house. Then Elizabeth and I got back to the task at hand: making dinner.

We got the beef in the oven and started boiling the potatoes. My goal was to have dinner ready when Elbert came home so I could speak to him without having to focus on the meal. Shortly thereafter, Matthew and Maria arrived, and we discussed what I was to do with all the new information. Matthew was shocked, and from a legal standpoint, he warned me that what Elbert did with the money could get me into trouble. I reminded him that Elbert had not shared his money with me. I was still using money from my parents, and he had never offered to help.

It seemed we had figured out the mystery of the treasure, but there was still one more enigma: Who was the lady Elbert was meeting with every night? Matthew offered to go to the tavern to find her and get more information.

This whole plan was centered on Elbert showing up for our dinner. I had not seen him all day, but Matthew saw him in town this morning. I asked if they had spoken, but they had not, as Elbert seemed in a rush. My friends and I strategized on how I could breach the subject of the treasure and came up with an idea: I would put a single gold coin on the table by his spot and wait for him to mention it. If by dessert he said nothing, I would say I found it while cleaning our room and was wondering where it came from. I wanted him to tell me his story; I knew he liked to spin a web of lies, but I had the truth already and would frame questions to get the whole story out of him.

At about four o'clock, Elizabeth would go home, Matthew would head to The Pickled Quail at six, and I would get ready for my evening with Elbert. At this time, my parents came down to the kitchen, letting me know they were on their way to the concert and not to stay up for them. My friends left after I promised to reconvene back in the kitchen later in the night. We reassured each other that we were doing the right thing. Soon, I was alone.

I went up to my room and dressed for the evening. I wanted to wear something strong and confident. Perhaps my clothes could convey what my heart was having difficulty saying. I searched through my wardrobe and found a red dress hidden in the back. I rarely wore it, but I felt confident every time I did. It was lined with black lace, and the neckline was slightly too low. It was something Mother never approved of, but it made me stand tall. I searched my jewelry box for an elegant necklace and found a red glass one to match. I felt more than ready for the night ahead. The chimes on the clock went off. It was six o'clock.

Downstairs, I triple checked that dinner was all set. I sat in the front hallway and kept an eye on the door and the clock. Had I told Elbert what time to be home? I could not remember. Soon the clock showed half past six and Elbert was not home yet. I went to the kitchen and brought all the food up to the table. As I brought up the last dish, the clock chimed seven, and Elbert walked through the door. I hurried to greet him and invited him into the dining room. He grunted and walked upstairs. I yelled that dinner was on the table and getting cold. He grunted again.

As we ate, there was not much conversation. "How was your day?"

"Pass the beef," he muttered.

"How are the seas today?" I tried again.

"It's the sea. What's it to you?"

After that, we ate in silence. I kept an eye on the coin by his spot, looking for any sign that he had noticed it. As we finished our main meal, I cleared his plate away and made a gesture toward the coin. He ignored my signal, so I went for the obvious. This was my opportunity. Before I picked up the coin, he saw me look at it from afar. I made sure of that. "Where did this come from?"

"Kathcrinc lcft it on thc table."

I rolled my eyes. "I know it isn't hers."

He continued with his lies, claiming it must have been my father who left it.

"It isn't his either. We both know that."

Elbert finally admitted that maybe the coin was his.

I understood now that my whole marriage was just another one of his deceptions. I had been oblivious, thinking love could change everything.

I went to the kitchen to bring up the blueberry pie,

and by the time I was back, the dining room was empty. I sat at the table with the pie and started to cry. I had married a dreadful man; he could not even stay for dessert. I found Peter and gave him the piece of pie I had promised. He saw my distress and wanted to know what happened. All I could get out was that something had ended. He offered comfort, but I left wanting not to disturb his evening. I went back to the kitchen to clean up from dinner, eager to hear if Matthew and Elizabeth had discovered anything at the tavern.

Chapter 30

The next day, Matthew, Elizabeth, Maria, and Teresa came down the backstairs into the kitchen. They found me at the sink trying to clean the dishes through puffy eyes. I had been crying all night.

Teresa embraced me in an enormous hug. "I thought something was off with him. He never seemed to be engaged with anyone but himself, like anytime I would see him in town, he would shy away from my attempts to say hello. I am sorry I should have spoken up earlier."

I assured her no apology was needed; we had all been deceived. I brought out the pie and some forks, and we sat at the kitchen table. I replayed the conversation I had with Elbert and shared that he had disappeared before dessert. Elizabeth shared more about the extent of his latest voyage after pressing harder on James for more information. She learned Elbert met up with his fellow Monahans to drink at a local tavern. While there, James found out that there was some controversy over Elbert leaving Ireland. The family did not elaborate, but James was warned that his captain was no good and had brought shame to their name.

I was not surprised anymore. If anything, I was numb. I did not think I could take anymore until Matthew cleared his throat and said he also had more information. I knew he had bad news. He could not look at me the whole time he was sitting there. It had to be bad. I needed a moment and suggested getting a bottle of sherry. Matthew jumped up to bring it over. As he left, I took a deep breath.

My girlfriends swarmed me, wanting to know how I was doing. I could not form a sentence. I just shook my head that I was okay, but no one believed that. Matthew returned with glasses and sherry, and we poured everyone a drink. He reached across the table, took my hands in his, and looked me deep in the eyes. I knew what this meant. He was about to shatter my world and wanted to comfort and support me. Suddenly, we heard the kitchen door creak.

My friends and I sat up straight and hid our drinks like school children, as if we felt we were in trouble for drinking in the kitchen. Maria offered to see who it was; she peeked out and came back with my parents. They were confused. Why were we all there? Where was Elbert? I turned to my friends to see if they thought it was a good idea to tell my parents what was going on, and they all nodded in agreement. I handed Mother and Father each a glass and invited them to sit down. We took turns telling them everything we knew: Elbert was a smuggler; he had a stash of gold coins and jewelry in our room; he lied so many times that we were still trying to piece together who he really was and why he wanted me as a wife.

Mother looked upset, Father looked angry, and Elizabeth, Teresa, and Maria looked nervous. I turned to Matthew. He stood up and moved next to me, took my hands again, and began his story.

"I went to the tavern to seek out the woman, but she was not there. I asked Mr. Jones if he knew her. He only knew her name, Siobhan, and that she came here from Ireland."

"So Elbert must know her from back home," I said.

"Well, I sat at the bar hoping she would show up, and I did not have to wait long. She took a seat at a table near the entrance. I approached and introduced myself as Zilla's lawyer who was looking for answers. She at first did not want to say who she was, but with some of my legal talk, she changed her tune."

"What did she say?" Elizabeth asked.

"Siobhan told me who Elbert really is: her husband. His name is not Elbert, but Robert."

"What?!" I blurted out.

"After she gave birth to their third child, Robert left with a promise to return with a fortune in the whaling industry. That was over five years ago. But then Robert went to Ireland on this last voyage. His family confronted him about leaving his wife and his children behind and discussed whether Siobhan should know that he had taken another wife and where he was. Ultimately, they felt she should know and even bought her a ticket to America. Siobhan's goal, she explained, was for Robert to support his children. She did not care if he came back, just that he would provide some financial help."

I couldn't believe what Matthew was saying.

"I assured her that none of us knew about Robert's background and that I would help her get him back to Ireland, where she could hold him accountable."

My Elbert was not even Elbert. He was already married, he had children. And he had denied me children! I looked around the room, scanning all who were sitting there. Father looked betrayed, Mother was outraged, my friends were as shocked as I was. The pieces had fallen into place, and it was making sense. I was a ploy to distract from his real life, to wash away his old responsibilities. I knew right then two things: he had to go, and I wanted revenge for what he did to me.

Maria and Teresa offered to stay the night, and I accepted. We slept in my old room so if Elbert came home, I would not have to see him. All in the kitchen agreed to meet back here the next morning to figure out a plan. Who knew that an evening meant for romance would end in such a way?

Chapter 31

Elbert did not return home that night, and I was filled with much relief. The next morning, my friends and I awoke ready to plan my revenge. We went to the dining room and had a quick breakfast with my parents. Then it was time to reconvene with everyone down in the kitchen. Katherine popped in too, even though she was off until Monday. We filled her in on what was going on. The details were shocking, she admitted, but she was not surprised, as she always thought he was shifty.

Matthew shared the news that he had invited Siobhan to come to the house so she could meet me and help with our plan. We knew Elbert would explain away anything we brought before him. We needed concrete proof to catch him in his lies, and Siobhan was an ideal resource. Soon she arrived and joined the team. Then Mother came in and presented an ingenious idea: a party.

"It's James' birthday this week! I was going to throw

a party. Why not do it that night?" exclaimed Elizabeth.

This would be the perfect cover. Elizabeth would invite James' friends to the party, which would include Elbert, and we would have Siobhan help bring out the cake. We also decided to don each of the women attending the party with a jewel from his stash. Mother offered to cook all the food and craved to be there when he figured out that his deceit was up. I was to relay the invitation to Elbert, impressing that it was important we attend. Siobhan was going to let him know she was busy that evening so he would not seek her out at the tavern. We all had our tasks and a week to make sure we were ready for the party.

During the following days, I pretended nothing had happened and focused on acting like a perfect wife. He had taken to being out all day and returning after I had gone to bed. On Wednesday, I approached him about the party. He grunted in disapproval, but I pressed its importance and highlighted that it was only one night, and James was his first mate. It would mean so much that he attended. "Isn't that what captains do?" I went over the guest list, omitting Siobhan, of course, and he agreed to go. I thanked him and kissed his cheek. He seemed none the wiser that his entire world was about to fall apart, much like mine had.

On Saturday morning, Mother and I packed all we needed for the party into the carriage. Katherine was eager to help for the evening, and Peter offered to be a footman. He had developed a hatred for Elbert, who had never had a nice word for him, just demands. It seemed everything Captain Elbert Monahan touched was tainted, and no one had a good word to say about him.

We arrived at Elizabeth's and went about setting up our ruse. With Maria, Matthew, and Teresa, our cast was set. It was in these moments I felt the most comfort, surrounded by loved ones. By the end of this evening, I would be free from Elbert. I prayed it all would go as planned.

Elizabeth invited us to her room, where we put on our best dresses. I had snuck multiple pieces of jewelry for us to wear. I picked a broach for myself. Maria picked a necklace, Elizabeth a ring, and Teresa a bracelet. We hoped he would notice and would be nervous that he was found out. We checked ourselves over in the mirror and collectively smiled. It was the first time in a while that I had smiled with such genuine ease. Our created family was my reason to smile today.

Siobhan arrived and came upstairs to check in. We had planned for her to stay upstairs until the right moment. Now all we had to do was wait. I had told Elbert to meet me at the party, as I had volunteered to help set up and was going to get ready there. I asked that he arrive at six o'clock, knowing he would not arrive until much later. At about half past five, guests arrived, and food and drinks started flowing. My friends and I were optimistic about our plan and enjoying ourselves. At six thirty, Elbert arrived. He looked disheveled, like he had forgotten he was coming to a party. Just another reason I needed to be rid of him.

I rushed up with a hug and a kiss. He smiled and went to find a drink. We mingled among the guests. Elbert kept staring at the jewelry my friends and I were wearing. He asked each one of them where it came from, to which they all answered that it was a gift from a good friend. At seven o'clock, act two of our plan went into play.

Siobhan, in a beautiful green dress and a giant diamond broach, walked in with Elizabeth, holding a giant birthday cake for James that Mother had baked. I traded my gaze between her and Elbert. He turned white upon seeing her and asked if we could leave. "We should stay," I said. "I'm having such a great time. We never go out, let's stay a bit longer!" He grabbed my arm and tried to force me out of the room. Matthew saw this action and stepped in to help. I pushed Elbert off. "Why are you so upset?" I waited to hear his next web of lies, and he did not disappoint. He claimed that the woman who brought out the cake was a former girlfriend who was stalking him. I snapped.

I grabbed his arm and pulled him into the kitchen. My friends and Siobhan followed as the rest of the guests continued to mingle and eat cake. I sat him down, then pulled out his loot from the cupboard, dumping all the coins and treasures on the table. I watched as his face went from anger to anxiety to disgust, his mind spinning, trying to come up with his next lie. He started mumbling, saying he could explain. I stopped him. This was my time. I had been betrayed; everyone in this room had been betrayed. I would not hear any more excuses. I wanted answers, and I was going to get them. I asked point blank, "Where did this come from?"

He stumbled again, looked around the room, and like an old sweater, he unraveled. He cried out, "You know me…I'm Elbert, the man you love. Don't you remember our walks on the beach, our love of sea glass? You are the one I want to be with!" With this, Siobhan stepped forward and asked him to tell the truth about who he really was. He looked between Siobhan and me, trying to decide whom he should play to keep his secret, but the two of us stood strong and the truth was his only choice. "I am Robert Monahan, and I fled my marriage to Siobhan because I did not want to be a father anymore."

Siobhan let out a cry. All I wanted to know was why. "Why?"

I could see the gears working in his head and waited in anticipation of his answer. He smiled as if he knew he had been bested but was still cocky about making it so long without getting caught. He threw up his hands and shouted, "You got me, I've been caught! You are all so clever!" His tone was one of sarcasm, with a tinge of fear. He asked for a whiskey, which Matthew handed him. He swallowed the whole glass in one gulp, wiped his face, and cleared his throat. "Five years ago, my third child in three years was coming, and I was done with all the yelling. Children are loud and messy, and I wanted nothing to do with that anymore. I made a promise to myself to get away from this life and start anew."

Siobhan shot him a look I had not seen in a long time, but knew it meant his inevitable demise.

"After the child's birth…" Elbert, well Robert, pointed at his first wife. "I convinced you that working at sea would be the great fortune we always talked about. I just never planned on coming home. When I arrived in Boston, I met a man who taught me how to smuggle goods, and found I was a natural at deceit. After learning all I could from him, I purchased the fastest ship I could and headed to Nantucket to build my new life. My first day on the island, the rest of the crews were returning, so I blended in with them. I knew enough about whaling that I could pass as a captain. I knew I had to cement myself here and what better way than to marry someone? I went into the tavern that night looking for a wife and knew I had little time to marry her before I would need to leave on my first voyage."

He swirled his glass, indicating he wanted more, to which Matthew shook his head. It would not be filled until he was done. Robert continued his story. "I saw you, Zilla, and you looked like someone I could easily make my wife, and you were very willing."

I shuddered and sat down, debating if I wanted to

hear anymore, but he continued before I could protest.

"I played up the role of whaling captain and hero, and everyone believed me."

Hearing him say it out loud made my blood boil, and I had to control myself from punching him.

He took a deep breath. "Once I found out you were the pastor's daughter, I knew you would make a great cover. Once I had my voyage and our wedding planned, I saw your house and felt that I would have a great place to hide my loot."

I heard Mother slam down a pot in the sink. I took a deep breath and quietly asked, with disdain in my voice, "Is there anything else you would like to confess?"

Robert swirled his glass again, and this time, Matthew obliged. After he swallowed the whole glass, he answered, "Just that you two are the most important women in my life!"

I could see through his manipulation. Siobhan and I gave each other a look. Neither of us believed him.

He then leaned in, took my hand and hers, and begged. "Please forgive me for my indiscretions. It was a mistake!"

Then Matthew stepped up and started talking about the legal ramification of smuggling, bigamy, fraud, and on and on. Robert was caught. And now he was begging not to be arrested. Matthew presented a contract for him to sign. In it, all the jewelry was to go to Siobhan, and all the gold coins were to go to me. As we were not legally married—being that he was still legally married to Siobhan—he was to move out of my parents' house immediately. I informed him that his things were already packed.

Siobhan said she did not want him to return, but he was to send her fifty percent of all earnings he made for the foreseeable future. Robert started to cry. He was also to return to Ireland, never to step foot on Nantucket again.

Robert asked for a pen and made a rude comment about being outsmarted by women. I presented the jewelry to Siobhan, and the coins were put in a fire bucket by the door. Matthew would accompany Robert to his ship to make certain of his departure. With a last attempt at bravado before leaving, Robert boasted, "I will regain my riches. This is not the last time the world will hear my name!"

I laughed and in jest yelled, "Which name would that be?" And with that, he walked out of my life forever, never to be heard from again.

Epilogue

Five Years Later

I took the gold coins and purchased a home for my parents so that Father could retire. Father handed over his flock to Arthur Smith and his family, sad about no longer being the pastor but excited about his new life. I keep in touch with Elizabeth and Maria, both of whom still live on the island. Elizabeth's husband now has his own ship, which an anonymous donor gifted him. He has left whaling and has become a lobsterman bringing in new fortune to his home. Maria fell in love with John, and I have just received word that they are to be married next month.

Matthew trained John and felt confident handing over his legal practice to him, returning to Taunton and his family business. Every Saturday, he joined for lunch with the family. After six months, he invited me out for a walk and asked if he could court me. I was ecstatic and accepted.

Matthew is the one who was always there for me, the one who genuinely cared.

We have just celebrated two years of marriage. We live in New Bedford, where he opened a second factory for the family. I had money to spare and wanted to start my own business, so I bought a tavern in town and asked Teresa and her husband to help me run it. They agreed to join my adventure, and the three of us work as partners; we seem to be successful.

> *There once was a woman from Nantucket,*
> *Who finally escaped with the bucket.*
> *And after a baffling affair,*
> *She completed a pair,*
> *And she yelled in happiness, I love it!*

About the Author

Karen Dropps holds a master's degree in Heritage Studies for a Global Society and a graduate certificate in Museum Studies from Regis College, Weston, Massachusetts. Karen followed adventurous careers in academia, museums, and cub scouts. She grew up in New England and now resides in the mountains of Colorado, where she enjoys skiing, hiking, and spending time with her family and cats.

www.ingramcontent.com/pod-product-compliance
Lightning Source LLC
Chambersburg PA
CBHW032004240626
47153CB00003B/1122